Crazy Loco

Stories by DAVID RICE

speak

An Imprint of Penguin Group (USA) Inc.

For my parents,
Rojelio y Maria

SPEAK
Published by Penguin Group
Penguin Group (USA) Inc.,
345 Hudson Street, New York, New York 10014, U.S.A.
Penguin Books Ltd, 80 Strand, London WC2R ORL, England
Penguin Books Australia Ltd, 250 Camberwell Road,
Camberwell, Victoria 3124, Australia
Penguin Books Canada Ltd, 10 Alcorn Avenue, Toronto, Ontario, Canada M4V 3B2
Penguin Books (N.Z.) Ltd, 182-190 Wairau Road, Auckland 10, New Zealand

First published in the United States of America by Dial Books,
a division of Penguin Putnam Inc., 2001
Published by Speak, an imprint of Penguin Group (USA) Inc., 2003

3 5 7 9 10 8 6 4

THE LIBRARY OF CONGRESS HAS CATALOGED THE DIAL EDITION AS FOLLOWS:
Rice, David, date.
Crazy Loco / stories by David Rice.
p. cm.
Summary: A collection of nine stories about Mexican American
kids growing up in the Rio Grande of South Texas.
ISBN: 0-8037-2598-1
1. Mexican Americans—Juvenile fiction. 2. Texas—Juvenile fiction.
[1. Children's stories, American. 2. Mexican Americans—Fiction.
3. Texas—Fiction. 4. Short stories.] I. Title.
PZ7.R36184 Cr 2001
[Fic]—dc21   00-059042

Printed in the United States of America

Speak ISBN 0-14-250056-9

❧ Acknowledgments ❧

Thanks to the Llano Grande Center for making available space and resources. I especially appreciate the students and staff for reading my drafts. Thanks also to the Edcouch-Elsa High School students for sharing their stories with me; they are my inspiration. And to Region One Education Service Center for inviting me to share stories with faculty and students across south Texas. And to my family and friends: Laura V. Rodríguez, Yvonne Guajardo, Father Sam Arizpe, Dr. Jaime Mejía, Dr. Luanne Brunson, Dr. Kent Reilly, Juan Rodríguez, John Wilson, Dr. Rolando Hinojosa-Smith, Daniel, Andrea, Macario, Mickey Yawn, Lisa Bell, Gastón Argüelles, Dr. Norman Peterson, Maria Eugenia Cotera, Christopher Caselli, Lauri Hornik, Carol, Renee, and Roger.

Contents

Sugarcane Fire

I have always liked older women. When I was a seventh grader, I had a crush on Verónica, an eighth grader, but she dated only high school guys. Her boyfriend was a sophomore and on the varsity football team. Verónica was the captain of the junior high cheerleaders, and since she liked football players, I joined the junior high team. The coach made me a water boy, and after a couple of games I realized that I should have joined the band. They got to sit and watch the game, and consequently had a good view of the cheerleaders, while I sat on the sidelines watching the other football players.

In April the junior high school held its annual spring dance. I went in hopes of dancing with Verónica, but she wasn't there. Apparently she attended only high school dances. The following week the high school would be having its spring dance, and I decided I'd go.

I tried to persuade two of my best friends, Estéban and

Riche, to come with me, but they said the high school students would make fun of us, or worse, beat us up. I told them that we had the right to go to any school dance or activity. Estéban laughed out loud and said, "Hello, we're in junior high. We have no rights." It took my PlayStation to convince them. If they came to the dance, they could borrow the PlayStation for three days—or one week if we got beat up.

I volunteered to walk over to the high school to buy the dance tickets, and my friends said they'd pay me later. The secretary at the front office told me the student council was selling the tickets, and she gave me directions to the room where they met. I walked down the hall feeling as if I didn't belong, but I reminded myself that in a couple of years I'd walk that hall every day.

There were about fifteen kids in the student council room, and I wasn't sure whom I should ask, so I spoke to the whole room. "Excuse me, I'd like to buy three tickets for the spring dance," I said.

The students all stared at me. There were two guys sitting across from each other playing poker, and one of them spoke up. "Are you in high school?"

"No," I said.

"What grade are you in?" the other one asked.

"Seventh," I said.

He tossed a penny into the pile in front of him. "What's your name?" he asked.

"Romero Ríos," I said.

A girl with wild curly hair and glossy red lips was sitting at a desk with a gray tin box in front of her. She leaned back in her chair and grinned at me. "This is a high school dance, not a junior high dance."

"I can go if I want. I have the right to go to any school dance or activity," I said.

One of the guys laughed. "You're in junior high. You have no rights." The other students joined in the ha-ha's.

Then I recognized the guy's laugh. A month earlier my English teacher had given the class extra-credit points for watching the high school drama club rehearse a Shakespeare play. Every time one of the actors messed up a line, the guy who was laughing at me now would jump in and make fun of him. And every time, the actor would throw his arms up and respond with the same sentence: "What is this? The Spanish Inquisition?" Then both guys would shout in unison, "Nobody expects the Spanish Inquisition," and all the actors would laugh. I didn't get it, but I knew it worked.

I threw my arms up. "What is this? The Spanish Inquisition?" I said.

The two poker players laughed and answered, "Nobody expects the Spanish Inquisition," and they let me buy three tickets. The girl with the tin box stood up and put out her hand. "That will be nine dollars for you and your dates," she said, smiling. I paid her and walked out happily.

Mom wouldn't let me wear a T-shirt to the dance. She said I should at least wear a shirt with a collar. She tried to make me wear a white shirt, but I told her I was going to a dance, not church. She bought me a blue one, and I barely got away without a tie.

The dance was at the high school gym from eight to twelve, and I told my friends we should meet there at eight-thirty to be fashionably late. They weren't out front when my parents dropped me off, so I waited outside a few minutes. I could hear the music, and I imagined myself dancing with Verónica.

I went inside, and the place was practically empty. There were a few guys leaning against the wall and a couple of teachers at the entrance. Two guys were selling sodas, popcorn, and pickles at a table in the lobby.

The gym was rather dim, lit only by the flashing colored lights the DJ had at his table. I walked across the basketball floor to the bleachers, where some girls were sitting in groups of three or four. I didn't see any guys on the bleachers, but I sat down anyway and carefully studied the girls' silhouettes while waiting for my friends. None of the girls looked like Verónica.

I decided to walk over to the concession stand to see if Estéban and Riche were leaning against the wall. They weren't. Just the same losers who were there when I arrived. I bought popcorn and a soda, then returned to my dark seat. I kept my eyes open for anyone I might know, but no one looked familiar. I ate my popcorn and drank my soda and began to worry that I looked stupid sitting by myself eating popcorn and drinking soda. I tried to seem as if

I were having fun, by tapping my feet and swaying slowly to the music. Then I worried that I didn't look cool, so I stopped swaying and tapping.

More kids I didn't know came into the gym, and some started dancing. A couple of girls were dancing with each other, and I thought maybe I should ask one of them, but my confidence was waning. Watching the light reflect off the waxed floors, I started to feel as if I didn't belong there. But I had to stick it out a little longer. I gave myself a time limit. I'd stay until ten-thirty. I finished my popcorn and soda and waited some more, and then I got up to buy another soda.

The lobby hadn't changed much. Guys were still leaning against the wall, but there were more kids walking around. I stood in the short line to order my soda and a pickle. I paid the guy and took a bite of my pickle, then turned around right into Verónica, her boyfriend, and the girl who had sold me the dance tickets. I chewed and swallowed as quickly as I could to say hi. Verónica sighed and gave me a tiny smile.

"Hey, Romero," she said. "What are you doing here?"

"Well, you know," I mumbled. I gave a small wave to her boyfriend and the ticket girl.

"Oh, this is Romero," she said. "This is my sister, Annette, and my boyfriend, Alfonso." She put her arm around her boyfriend.

I held out my hand to her sister. "Hi, I'm Romero Ríos." Annette shook my hand and held it a little longer than I was used to. I tried to gently pull back, and I felt her give my hand a squeeze before she let go. Blushing, I looked down and noticed that she had a tattoo of a red flower on her ankle.

"I know who you are. I sold you the tickets," Annette said in a singsong voice. "So, where are your dates? Don't you have a girlfriend?"

"He doesn't have a girlfriend," Verónica announced merrily.

"Who did you come with?" Alfonso asked.

"Myself," I said.

"This is a high school dance, not a junior high dance," Alfonso said.

"I have a right to be here," I answered. "Verónica is here and she's in junior high."

Alfonso stepped toward me. "Yeah, but she's my date. I invited her. Who invited you?"

Annette rolled her eyes. "Okay, Mr. Macho," she said to Alfonso. "Why don't you find us a place to sit?"

"See ya round, Romero," Annette said as they walked away. Alfonso had his arm around Verónica and a finger tucked into her belt loop.

I walked over to where the guys were leaning against the wall and took my place. After a minute I felt like a loser, and then I felt like a bigger loser for *thinking* I was a loser, and then I felt like a *gigantic* loser for leaning against the wall with a bunch of losers. I pushed off the wall, threw my soda and pickle in the trash, and walked home.

My parents and little sister and brother were watching a video when I walked in.

"Hey, mi'jo, how did you get home?" Dad asked, looking concerned.

"I walked."

"You could have called, you know. We would have picked you up," he said.

"Your friends didn't show up, did they?" Mom asked.

I shook my head. "Bunch-a losers."

"They called. They said their parents wouldn't let them go," Mom told me.

"Yeah, whatever," I said. "I'm going to bed."

"Aren't you hungry?" Dad asked. "There's some caldo on the stove. It's good. Your mama Locha made it."

"Nah, I'm full of popcorn."

"Well, how about we all go to Dairy Queen for chocolate-dip cones?" he said.

My brother and sister leaped up and started shouting, "Dairy Queen! Dairy Queen!"

"You guys go ahead," I said.

Mom put her hand on my shoulder. "I'll share french fries and a chocolate sundae with you." She always said the right thing.

Over the summer I didn't see Verónica. I heard she was in San Antonio with her cousins. I had cousins in San Antonio too, but I didn't like them enough to spend my whole summer with them in hopes of running into Verónica. Besides, she was going to be a freshman in the fall, and I would still be stuck in junior high.

A couple of weeks before school started, Mom took me to the mall to buy new jeans. After shopping we ate burgers at the food court and watched the people walk by. Mom and I talked about the coming school year, what my plans were. While I was talking, I noticed Mom looking over to my side. I turned. There stood Verónica's sister, Annette.

"Hi, Romero," she said. I felt my cheeks turn red.

I stood up and introduced her to my mother, and Annette was charming. She said "yes, ma'am" with respect, and "thank you" with sincerity each time Mom commented on how pretty she was. On the way home Mom asked lots of questions about her. I explained how Annette was about to be a senior in high school and was way out of my league, but I found myself thinking about her for the rest of the day. Verónica was still the one, though.

Eighth grade went well for me right away. I was elected student council historian, and I began attending drama club meetings. I decided to try my hand at acting and forget about football. On Friday nights my friends and I attended the high school football games, much like the whole town, and I watched Verónica jump and shout for her new boyfriend, Freddy—or Fast Freddy, if you were his friend.

At one of the games, a week before homecoming, the captain of the cheerleaders announced over the loudspeaker that they were selling tickets for a hayride to raise money for the homecoming dance. Estéban turned to me. "Another high school dance you can go to, Disco Boy."

At halftime the cheerleaders and the pom-pom squad came through the stands selling the hayride tickets. Verónica walked up my aisle, and I reached into my pocket for two dollars.

"What are you doing?" Estéban asked. "You're not buying a ticket to the hayride, are you?"

"Sí, señor," I said.

Verónica stepped up beside me and I held out my two dollars. She looked at me and put her hands on her hips. "Romero, this is a high school hayride," she said.

I kept my two dollars out. "I'll buy one ticket, please."

She sighed, then slowly took my two dollars, keeping her eyes on me, trying to stare me down or something. I smirked as she put a ticket in my hand. "Thank you," I said.

"Whatever," she grumbled, and she walked off, shaking her head.

"Fast Freddy is going to kill you," Riche said.

"You don't know Fast Freddy well enough to call him Fast Freddy," I answered.

The night of the hayride was cool, and a harvest moon shined down from above. As I waited to get into one of the two caged trailers filled with hay bales, I looked around and noticed that everyone seemed to have a date. Everyone except me. We were herded into the trailers, and I followed my flock into the second one. Hay and dust were being kicked up everywhere. I searched for Verónica but didn't see her.

Then I did: She was standing by her boyfriend's car. She opened the car door and got in, and they drove off. I turned to get out of the cage, but the sheep wouldn't move, and anyway, where would I go? Home, and then to Dairy Queen.

I sat down on a hay bale in a front corner of the cage and tried to find someone I knew. No one. Not a soul. They were all strangers. In front of me was the truck that pulled our trailer. We began to move and then stopped with a jolt. The red taillight was suddenly blinding, and I turned away. The back gate opened up, and I thought about escaping, but it slammed closed too quickly and the trailer started moving again.

I discovered that the front of the cage wasn't the best place to sit. Loose hay flew all around, and when we veered off the farm road, I had to cover my face to keep dust out of my eyes and nose. As we drove I focused on the white lines on the road. The taillights' glow, soothing now that the brakes weren't on, blurred in my mind into disco lights reflecting off a waxed wooden floor, and I thought to myself, "What am I doing here?"

We came to another stop, and a light tap on my shoulder brought me back to the hayride. Even in the glare of the brake lights, I could tell that it was Annette. The light made a halo around her curls and gleamed off her glossy lips. "Hi, Romero," she said, her voice cocky. "Can I sit next to you?"

I stood up, feeling disoriented. "Oh, hi, Annette," I said. "How are you?"

"Well, can I sit here?" she asked again.

"Yes, if you want," I mumbled.

"Thank you," she said—and then something else, but I couldn't hear.

"What?" I said.

She sat and pulled me down next to her. "I said, what are you doing here?"

"What do you mean?" I answered.

She pushed her hair to one side. "I mean, what are you doing here? This is a high school hayride. I'm a senior. You're . . . what? An eighth grader?"

I leaned toward her. "I can be here if I want."

"Oh, that's right," she teased. "You like to have rights."

The truck pulled us off the main farm road and onto a smaller road. We were moving more slowly now and could talk without shouting. Annette's long hair blew around her face, and her brown eyes caught the reflection of the disco lights. She moved a little closer to me, and I could feel her thigh touching my thigh. I thought I should probably move, but I was already against the cage.

"So why *are* you here?" Annette asked. "Looking for my sister?"

"No, I'm not looking for anyone," I said. "I like supporting my school." She nodded and smiled.

"Why are *you* here?" I said.

"I have a right to be here if I want," she said, mimicking me. "I can do whatever I want."

We didn't talk for a moment, and I could feel her thigh pressing against mine, but I was afraid to press back.

11

She leaned toward me and whispered in my ear, "I followed you here."

"Wh-what did you say?" I stuttered.

"The moon is *soooo* big tonight. It must be a full moon," she said. "The full moon makes me crazy."

"It's the harvest moon," I said.

"Looks full to me. I'll bet there are demons out tonight." She pressed her thigh to mine a little harder, and I could feel her body heat.

We were passing sugarcane fields when the brake lights came on again. Everyone stood up on the hay bales, and we could see a fire up ahead. Fire engines were off to the side of the road, and police officers were directing traffic. Firefighters were spraying water on the sugarcane fields. We could hear shouts from the police and our drivers, but we couldn't make out what they were saying. Annette was standing behind me. I felt her chest against my back, and her hand brushed my hand. She lightly stroked my arms with her fingernails, and I got goose bumps all over me. Then she gently rubbed my hands with her fingertips and held them firmly.

"What do you think is going to happen?" she asked.

"I don't know," I said.

I wasn't sure what to do. Maybe Annette was holding my hands because she was scared or maybe because she liked the way it felt. She pressed her body to mine, and I gently pressed back. I could feel her chest against my shoulder.

"What's going to happen to us?" she whispered, her warm breath in my ear.

"I think we'll be fine, but it's dangerous," I said in a hushed tone.

"What do you mean?" she asked as we pressed our bodies together.

"Well, everything here is flammable. One spark and we'll catch fire," I said.

We moved slowly beside the field. Ashes floated in the blurred sky as the flames climbed around the cane. There was a sweet, dark scent to the air. It smelled like church during confessional. The sweet smoke was making my heart beat faster, and I became dizzy. I closed my eyes and felt Annette's hands on my waist, felt her turning me and wrapping her arms around me. The truck stopped and I opened my eyes to find Annette in front of me, surrounded in a red glow. She pulled herself closer and her hips pressed against mine. She kissed me. I didn't move. I inhaled deeply and the sugar swirled in my head. Her tongue licked my lips, and all I could hear was the fire cracking the sugarcane.

Her Other Son

When I was growing up in the Rio Grande Valley of south Texas, there was never a time when we didn't have a live-in maid working for us. You see, we were rich. Most families who had maids paid them only twenty-five dollars a week. We paid ours thirty-five dollars a week. Our maid, Catalina, was always telling my brother and me how lucky we were to have such a big beautiful home.

Our white frame house had five whole rooms. The kitchen had a gas stove and a sink and shelves filled with assorted colors of plastic cups and plates. The one bathroom, which also served as the family closet, was always warm because one wall doubled as the back of the refrigerator. Our grandfather had his own bedroom complete with a TV! After all, it was his house we lived in. The fourth room was a bedroom where Mom, Dad, and my brother and I all slept. Our parents had a double bed, and my brother and I had bunk beds. I slept on top. The last room was the living room, which was actually an extension of the family bedroom and also served as Catalina's bedroom during the week. She slept on the couch, though how she fit was a bit of a wonder, since she was a little on the chubby side.

Sometimes late at night I'd wake up and look down at everyone from my bunk bed. Dad would be holding Mom closely, and under me, my brother would be sleeping with his mouth wide open. I also had a clear view of Catalina on the living room couch, because no walls nor even a curtain divided the two rooms. Deep rhythms of comfort and peace would fill me as I watched the silhouettes gently inhaling and exhaling.

I did sometimes imagine what it would be like to have my own room. In our house there was no privacy. Mom liked to tease Dad about how the whole house could hear him when he went to the bathroom. Dad would laugh, not a bit embarrassed. "At least you *have* a bathroom," Catalina would say. Catalina's house in Mexico didn't have indoor plumbing, as Mom often reminded us. My brother, George, and I would shrug our shoulders and say, "So what? Grandma's house in Weslaco has an outhouse. You don't see her complaining all the time." We'd mimic Catalina and Mom would whack on the head whoever was closest.

We'd never been to Catalina's house in Mexico because there was no reason to go. We didn't have to pick her up or anything. Catalina came in on Monday mornings and left on Friday afternoons. Mom and Dad drove her to Weslaco, Mom's hometown, and Catalina took a bus from there to Las Flores, México.

Las Flores was really a border town named Nuevo Progreso, and it had lots of stores where you could buy things more cheaply than on the U.S. side. People called it Las Flores because at night women in tight flower-print dresses lined the streets, trying to pick up men and charge them a few dollars for their company. Mom said that Catalina's daughter was one of these women. "Why doesn't she do something else?" I asked. Mom said there were no jobs in Las Flores. It was either work in a maquiladora earning pennies an hour, be a maid, or—if you were pretty enough—work at night.

Catalina didn't talk much about her daughter, who Mom said had abandoned her sons. The boys lived with Catalina, their grandmother, as well as with Catalina's parents. George and I couldn't imagine Catalina having a mother and father, but Mom told us that Catalina's father was older than our grandfather, and still walked everywhere. Our grandfather couldn't walk without a walker.

Catalina often told us how much we reminded her of her grandsons. She'd bring her hands gently together and say how we were such cute boys and how one day we'd be handsome men and all the girls would chase us. At the time that was the last thing we wanted.

Until I was fifteen years old, Catalina was our maid, but she acted more like an older aunt. She'd even take care of

George and me if we got sick. At the start of every school year I'd get terrible headaches, probably from nerves. But Catalina said it was from mal de ojo. I'd come home with a headache, and Catalina would say it was because a girl had put a curse on me.

"You're so handsome that all the girls want to meet you," she'd say. "If you're too shy to smile at them, they'll curse you. And make sure you shake their hands or touch their shoulder too."

She'd have me lie down on the couch dressed only in my underwear, and she'd roll an egg all over my body, from head to toe. Standing next to the couch she'd then roll the egg between her palms while praying in Spanish under her breath. On my forehead and chest and on every joint she would make the sign of the cross with the egg, and it felt good to listen to her soothing voice and be tickled by the cool, smooth egg. After a few minutes she would stop and break the egg into a glass half filled with water, to see the results. If the whole egg lay at the bottom of the glass intact, all I had was a regular headache, but if the egg white floated to the top, I had been a victim of El Ojo. The white always rose to the top. Eventually I took Catalina's advice and started greeting girls with a smile and a friendly handshake.

Over the years, whenever George and I outgrew our clothes, they were put in big plastic bags for Catalina to take home with her on the weekends. She took Mom and Dad's old clothes too. And if Mom bought a new lamp or some other home furnishing, the old one became Catalina's.

One day Dad came home with a fifty-five-gallon barrel. He worked at a chemical plant where they sold pesticides to farmers and crop duster pilots. When he brought home the red steel drum, he took the lid off and poured gasoline down the inside walls, then set it on fire to get rid of all the poison. George and I were amazed by the bright blue flames. Once the fire was out, Dad poured in water and a whole bottle of dishwashing soap and stirred it up with a broomstick. He let it sit for a while and then rinsed it out with the garden hose. We begged Dad to let us play in the barrel, but he said Catalina's family was going to use it as a shower. My brother and I laughed, and then Mom whacked my head, which made my brother laugh harder.

Occasionally our mother and tías drove Catalina home, because Mom and the tías loved to shop in Las Flores. They'd return with candy and cookies for us, and sometimes a blanket or a brightly colored piggy bank, which we'd break in two weeks or so. But George and I didn't like going to Mexico. Though we had grown up listening to Spanish all our lives, we didn't speak the language very well, and we were a little afraid of crossing the border. There were always all these mean-looking men with guns on both sides of the border, and they never took off their sunglasses. We'd go over to Mexico to shop, and when we came back across the bridge, a border patrol agent always leaned toward the window and asked us if we were all American citizens.

Before we got to the checkpoint, Mom would coach us:

"When the man asks if we're all American citizens, you say, 'Yes, sir.'" Once, when I was eight years old, I'd been too nervous to answer. The border patrol agent said in a stern voice, "Son, are you an all-American citizen?" and I couldn't speak. My father turned to look at me, and said, "Tommy, tell the man, 'Yes, sir.'" I stared out the car window at a family that looked like us; the border patrol was searching their car. And I looked at the chain-link fences with razor wire on top and then at my reflection in the border patrol agent's dark sunglasses, and I shook my head. He didn't say anything, but he raised his brow, and then Dad said, "He is my son, and we have been here a lot longer than you have."

"I'm sorry, sir, what was that?" the agent asked, furrowing his brow. Mom nudged Dad with her elbow.

Dad clenched the steering wheel and looked toward the sign saying WELCOME TO TEXAS. Then he looked back at the agent and said, "He is my son and you're scaring him."

The agent gave me another glance, stood upright, then waved his hand. "Move along," he said.

Every weekend Catalina made the trip across the border, and I wondered if she went through the same ordeal. She had a visitor's visa and could stay for a week at a time, but only in the Valley. She wasn't allowed to go past the second checkpoint, which was in Falfurrias, a town sixty miles from the first checkpoint. I imagined that each time she crossed, the agents searched her bags. All I knew was that every time *I* crossed the border, I feared that they wouldn't let me come back home.

When it was photo day at school, Mom made us wear nice shirts, and Catalina always commented on how handsome we looked. She'd ask for copies of the pictures, and Mom always gave them to her. Catalina said she put them up in her house, which didn't make any sense to George and me. After all, she wasn't family or anything, and we didn't have any pictures of her on our walls.

Each time Mom gave her a picture, she would stare at it and marvel. I think that's what made Mom and Dad buy her a 35-mm pocket camera one Christmas. When she opened the box and saw that it was a camera, her eyes got misty. She wasted one whole roll of film on us opening presents under our artificial silver Christmas tree. I bet she took more than a thousand pictures of us through the years. Mom would give her a roll of film with every paycheck, and Catalina would get them developed at a pharmacy in Weslaco.

When I was twelve, Mom and Dad built a brand-new house for the family, a few blocks from our old home. It was a big white brick house with four bedrooms—the perfect size for us. There were bedrooms for everyone: one for Grandfather, one for Mom and Dad, one for George, and one just for me. But that's not how it worked out. Catalina got her own bedroom, and George and I had to share. Of course I threw a bit of a fit and got whacked on the head by Mom.

The move was exciting, though, and Mom bought lots of new furniture for the house. We got new bunk beds and a chest of drawers, lamps, a sofa, a La-Z-Boy, and a kitchen table and chairs. Catalina took her pick of all the old furniture, and Dad and a friend of his hauled all the old stuff to Catalina's house. Everyone was happy, and George and I divided up our bedroom so nicely that our parents rewarded us with our own private phone line.

Two years later Dad got a job that required lots of traveling to San Antonio. During one of his trips, he brought Mom, Grandfather, George, and me along to visit our tía Carmen and tío Lali. George and I were happy to visit them because our six cousins were older than us and could drive us around the city.

Catalina was happy about our visit too, because we had to drive through Falfurrias to get there. Just north of Falfurrias was Don Pedrito Jaramillo's shrine. Pedrito Jaramillo was a curandero born in Mexico; it was said that he had cured a man when he was only eight. Catalina carried a small picture of Pedrito Jaramillo in her purse. She would always take it out and place it beside me when she cured me of El Ojo. Before our trip she asked Mom if we would stop at the shrine and buy her a bigger picture to hang on the wall in her home.

Catalina had always wanted to visit Don Pedrito Jaramillo's shrine, but she couldn't because just nine miles south of it, on Highway 281, was a border patrol checkpoint. Catalina's visitor's visa wouldn't allow her to travel past Falfurrias. She said that the border patrol did it on purpose to keep the Mexican people from praying at the shrine. So on the way back from San Antonio we stopped at the shrine and walked around. It was a very strange place: a small concrete building with a three-foot-high chain-link fence around it and a few graves in front belonging to the people who used to own the land. Inside, the shrine was warm and dim, with hundreds of lit velas making the walls glow.

The walls were covered with handwritten letters and photos of people and even pets. Most of the letters were written in Spanish, asking Don Pedrito for his healing powers. Next to the shrine was a small store that sold little statues of Don Pedrito Jaramillo, bottles of holy water, and velas. Mom bought Catalina the picture she had asked for, and a vela with Don Pedrito Jaramillo's face on it. She also took photos of the shrine, using Catalina's camera. Catalina was so pleased that she put one of the photos up in her bedroom in our house along with the picture of Don Pedrito Jaramillo.

Toward the end of my sophomore year Dad got a job offer in Austin, and we were told over a sneak-attack dinner that we'd be moving at the end of the month. Dad had already found a house and had checked out the school nearby. Mom and Dad went on about the opportunities we had before us, but it was difficult to listen. George, his eyes looking down at his plate, seemed to be searching his rice and beans for a way to keep us in Edcouch.

"What about Catalina?" he said. "We can't just leave her here, and they won't let her past Falfurrias."

Mom gave him an understanding smile. "Mi'jo, Catalina's

home is in Las Flores. She has grandchildren to take care of. Her family is there."

George scowled at me and I clued in. "What about Grandfather? Someone has to take care of him, and we can't because we'll be in school."

Dad looked at Mom, and I could sense that they had all the answers. "Your grandfather can take care of himself during the day," Dad said. "And besides, you two are old enough to help your mother bathe and shave him in the evenings."

It was a somber month for George and me. Catalina seemed unhappy too, but then she had some grave concerns of her own. Her younger grandson, Guillermo, was very sick. Mom, who worked as an X-ray technician at the hospital in Weslaco, had taken a trip to see him and then talked to one of the doctors at her hospital about his symptoms. The doctor prescribed some medicine and threw in free samples and lots of advice. During the last week we were in Edcouch, Catalina stayed in Mexico trying to nurse her grandson back to health, but we were so busy packing for the move that we didn't even talk about it.

One day Mom and Dad took a trip to Austin to sign papers on a house, and Mom decided to make a stop at Don Pedrito Jaramillo's shrine. She had a photo of Catalina's grandsons, and though she wasn't sure who was who, she wanted to put the picture on the wall and say a prayer for Guillermo. I had seen the picture and didn't think the boys looked anything like George and me, but I'd recognized the shirts they were wearing.

By the time Mom and Dad came home, George and I had finished packing. Our parents were so surprised at what a good job we'd done that they said they'd take us out for pizza to celebrate and to tell us all about the new house. Dad winked at us. "You'll each have your own bedroom," he said.

George and I gave each other high fives. "Yes!" we shouted. But as we were leaving the house, we got a call from Catalina.

It was clear from Mom's expression as she talked on the phone that the news wasn't good. When she hung up, we weren't surprised to hear her say that Catalina's grandson had died. "The funeral is tomorrow morning," Mom told us with a shake of her head.

George leaned over to me and whispered, "You know what that means." And I did.

The next day I was stuck riding across the border to Las Flores with Mom and my tía. The funeral was scheduled for ten o'clock at a cemetery on the outskirts of town. Somehow Dad and George had weaseled out of going, but I didn't have their luck.

Once we crossed the river to Las Flores, my mom and tía, both wearing black veils, spoke only in Spanish. I understood most of what they said, but didn't pay too much attention. They always spoke more Spanish than English, but in Mexico they could be entirely themselves.

24

The cemetery was a dried-out place. We joined the small group of people gathered around the grave, all dressed in black. When Catalina saw us, she began to cry.

I felt deeply sorry for the woman, but it was difficult to express myself in Spanish. She gave me a big hug and murmured, "Qué lindo." She asked for George and my dad, but Mom explained that they had to load the truck for the move to Austin. Catalina looked as if she were going to cry again, but then she simply said, "God will watch over them."

There was a boy with her, and she introduced us. He was Emiliano, Guillermo's older brother. He was my height and had on my old clothes. They fit him perfectly. Suddenly I could see why Catalina thought he looked like me. Her parents, who were old and frail, were there too; her mother began to cry when she saw me. She hugged me and said in Spanish, "One of the other sons."

As it turned out, the family had walked to the cemetery, so Mom offered the adults a ride back to their house. Emiliano and I were stuck walking. I sensed that he wanted to talk, but I wasn't confident in my ability to carry on a conversation. My Spanish was very Tex-Mex, and I thought he probably would laugh at me. For the first mile or so to his house, we didn't say a word. Finally he slowed down, stopped, and looked at me. He held out the sides of his shirt and asked me if it had been mine. I said yes, but that it looked better on him. He laughed.

We walked some more, and then he said he had seen pictures of me wearing the same shirt. That's how he knew that it used to be mine. I smiled, then wondered what Guillermo had looked like in George's clothes. I told him I was sorry about his brother, and he shrugged his shoulders and said nothing.

All at once I spotted our silver car in front of a tiny shack. All of the houses in the neighborhood were the same, but I couldn't believe this was Catalina's home. I felt guilt start to stir inside me.

Emiliano opened the door for me, and I walked straight into my old house in Edcouch! There was my old bunk bed against the wall, and across the room was my parents' old double bed. Everything in this house had been in ours at one time. Tacked onto the walls were at least a hundred photographs.

There were pictures of George and me through the years, and pictures of Catalina's grandsons, wearing our clothes and smiling in every shot. Catalina walked up to me and said, "You see, you and George look so much like my grandsons." Then she started sobbing. "Thank God your mother bought me that camera. Now I'll have pictures of Guillermo to carry all my life."

Mom put her arm around Catalina and had her sit down on the bed, and Emiliano gestured for me to follow him outside. We walked through the kitchen, where our old cups and plates were stacked on shelves. On the table were the bottles of pills prescribed for Guillermo by the doctor at my mother's hospital.

Once outside, Emiliano picked up a soccer ball and

kicked it to me. I kicked it back. I noticed the red barrel
had wanted so much as a kid. It was set atop a wooden tri
pod and had one of our old shower curtains strung around
its base.

Emiliano and I kicked the ball around for a while, and
then Catalina and my mother and tía came outside. Catalina had her camera and asked Emiliano and me to pose
next to each other. He put his arm around me and I smiled

We said our good-byes, and Mom told Catalina that we
would keep in touch and let her know each time we were
coming down. I shook hands with Emiliano and he gave
me a hug. As we drove off, they stood outside and waved.
My tía commented that Emiliano and I looked like brothers, and for the first time I didn't mind the comparison.

The Mexican border agents let us pass with no problem,
and we crossed over the concrete bridge that was lined with
barbed wire. I looked out over the Rio Grande and saw kids
playing along the shore on the Mexican side. A patrol car
with tinted windows drove slowly along the U.S. side.

As we moved in stop-and-go fashion to the checkpoint, I
thought about Emiliano and Guillermo. How they had
known about us all this time while we didn't have a clue,
much less an interest, in them. How they wore our clothes
and slept in our beds. And probably included us in their
prayers. And then how I'd been called one of the other sons.

The border patrol agent held up his hand, and my
mother stopped the car. He placed his hand on the roof and
leaned in. We couldn't see his eyes through his dark sun-

glasses as he asked if we were all American citizens. Mom and my tía smiled and nodded, saying yes over and over. He turned his head slightly and said to me, "And you? Are you an all-American citizen?"

I didn't answer.

Valentine

My kindergarten teacher didn't teach us about love. She taught us how to be polite, how to share, and to say please and thank you. Not a word about love. But my first-grade teacher, Ms. de los Santos, brought up the subject one week before Valentine's Day.

"Valentine's Day," she explained to us, "is the day for showing the person you love just how much you love them. It's the day you express your love by giving them flowers, candy, cards . . . or anything you want, as long as it comes from your heart."

"How do you know who you love?" I asked. She said it was the person you thought of the most, and for me, that was Nina.

Nina had been in my kindergarten class and was now in my first-grade class as well. She was beautiful. I would play house with her and even play with dolls, just to be close to her. On the playground, I pushed her on the swing whenever she asked. I followed her everywhere. And it paid off, because sometimes she would hang upside down on the monkey bars, wearing a dress.

The day before Valentine's Day I begged my mother to take me to Globe, the big department store in McAllen, to buy Valentine cards. Globe had a huge card section. Mom bought me a box of Scooby-Doo valentines for my school friends, but I wanted a special card for Nina. They had cards for mothers, fathers, wives, husbands, aunts, uncles, sisters, brothers, grandmothers, and grandfathers. Cards for everyone except Nina. No card said BE MY VALENTINE, NINA.

Then I found one with a shiny red embossed heart on it. The heart was bigger than my hand. My little fingers gently glided over the heart, and I could feel that this was the perfect card for Nina. I imagined her fingers touching the card the way I was doing, and it made me forget to breathe.

My mom said that the card was too expensive and that I should give Nina a Scooby-Doo valentine. But I told her Nina was special. "She's my best friend," I said. Mom took the card in her hands and let her fingers glide over the heart, and she grinned, then winked at me. When we got home, she helped me write inside the card, "Be my valentine, Nina." That night I dreamed of Nina holding my card close to her heart.

Ms. de los Santos had the whole room decorated for our Valentine's Day party. She loved to throw parties. For

Thanksgiving she had all of us Mexican American kids dress up like Pilgrims. We didn't get it, but we liked wearing the costumes. For Halloween we made scary masks and ate candy apples. At our Christmas party we made elf hats, ate buñuelos, and learned to sing "Jingle Bells." The song didn't make much sense to us. Dashing through the snow in a one-horse open sleigh? It never snowed in the Rio Grande Valley. Well, maybe during the Ice Age.

Now for Valentine's Day, big red cardboard hearts with our names on them were taped to the walls. Mine was at the bottom and was bent, but there were three gold stars next to my name. Several red cardboard cupids hung from the ceiling. Each cupid had a bow and arrow, and all had their bows pulled back, aiming love arrows at the lucky people of the world. In the back of the room, waiting for hungry mouths, was a chocolate cake with the red frosting words BEST WISHES ON VALENTINE'S DAY.

The party began with the exchange of valentines. I gave Ms. de los Santos a heart-shaped box of chocolates that my mother had bought at Globe, and she hugged me and gave me a Sweet Tart heart that said CUTIE. I did look cute, I think. I had on a red shirt, and it matched Nina's red valentine dress.

I passed out my cards, saving Nina's for last. Slowly I approached her, the big valentine hidden behind me. Then I put out my arm and held the card in front of her. She smiled and said to put it in her bag, but I wanted her to take it in her hands and open it right away.

I told her it was a special card. She shook her bag and the other cards fluttered. "Drop it in the bag," she said.

I kept my arm out. "I wrote something special in your card," I said.

She sighed. "Drop it in the bag," she said. I let my card fall onto the top of her stack of valentines, but it was so heavy that it sank to the side and then to the bottom of the stack. She snapped the bag shut and walked off. I could feel my heart bending and folding.

Once we were all seated, Ms. de los Santos called our names one by one to get our cookies, punch, and chocolate cake. Across from my chair, to my right, were Bobby and Marco, my best friends in the class. They were bigger than I was, and always helped me up the monkey bars or pushed me really high on the swing. But they were always up to something: punching pinholes in other kids' milk cartons, shooting spitballs through straws, or worse, catching tiny bugs and shooting *those* through the straws into kids' hair.

Nina sat in front of Bobby, and as she passed between us to take her seat, Bobby and Marco reached out with their pencils and lifted up her dress. I could see her white lace panties. I had seen them before when she hung upside down on the monkey bars, but this was different.

She whipped around and looked right at me, her eyes filled with hurt. She began to cry and ran to our teacher. Ms. de los Santos said, "Ay, mi'jita, qué te pasó?" Through her breaking voice Nina said that I had lifted her dress. Now *my* eyes were filled with hurt. Ms. de los Santos raised her brow, and all the girls turned to me and glared. The boys in the class clenched their fists, and I could see that this was their chance to prove their love for Nina. Bobby and Marco smirked at me.

Ms. de los Santos leaned back in her chair and put her hands together. "Luis, did you lift up Nina's dress?" she asked.

I couldn't answer. Nina was nodding, and I shook my head in disappointment that she believed I would do such a thing.

"Luis, I'm asking you a question. Did you lift up Nina's dress?" Ms. de los Santos repeated.

I looked at Nina and at Ms. de los Santos and shook my head. "No, Ms. de los Santos. It wasn't me."

"Do you know who did it?" she asked.

I turned to Bobby and Marco, hoping they would admit their actions, but they just kept smirking. I knew then that I had to tell the truth, to tattle on my friends. But no one likes a tattletale.

"Luis, answer me, please. Do you know who did?"

I looked at Bobby and Marco again and nodded. They squinted at me and leaned slightly forward, ready to pounce. I began to have second thoughts, but I glanced at Nina, who looked sad, her eyes still watering.

"Luis, mi'jito, tell me who did it," Ms. de los Santos said.

My body felt weak. I gripped the sides of my desk for strength and turned to look at my bent heart on the wall, three shiny stars by my name. I turned back to Bobby and

Marco and hoped they would decide for me. They did: They said nothing.

"Luis?" Ms. de los Santos said again.

I stood up and pointed. "It was Bobby and Marco," I said loudly so the whole class could hear.

They quickly began with, "No, Ms., it wasn't us, it was him. We didn't do nothing." Their lies were not heard.

Ms. de los Santos made them go up to her desk, and she rose before them. "I'm so disappointed in you boys," she said. "How would you like it if I lifted up your dress?" Bobby and Marco chuckled.

"That's it. You boys get no cookies or punch, and Luis gets your pieces of cake. How do you like that?"

They didn't. They turned to me with revenge in their eyes. Ms. de los Santos made them pick up their pieces of chocolate cake and place them on my desk, and they glared at me. Nina sat in her chair without giving me so much as a smile. My heart sank a little, but I took a bite of chocolate cake, and chocolate cake makes you forget everything.

The next day Nina didn't talk to me, Bobby and Marco didn't play with me, and all the students in the class were cool toward me, but I didn't know why. I had done what was right. Bobby and Marco, my former best friends, were now my school bullies, and they didn't let a day go by without doing their best to make me uncomfortable. If I played marbles, they kicked them or stomped them into the dirt. On the playground they knocked me off the monkey bars. In the cafeteria line they bumped me to make me drop my tray, and a couple of times they were successful. Once Nina saw them knock over my tray, but she just joined the others and laughed. Only Ms. de los Santos knew what Bobby and Marco were up to, so after first grade I had no one to watch over me.

I thought elementary school was tough, but matters got worse in junior high. I had to ride the bus with Bobby and Marco, and I can't count the times they tried to trip me as I walked down the aisle to my seat. They glued my locker padlock shut a few times, and once they managed to tie fishing line from my belt loop to my chair so that when I stood up, the chair came with me. The teacher blamed *me* for that one, as if I would tie myself to my chair. One time they even kidnapped my dog Fluffy and dyed him pink, but for that they got in big trouble. My mom loved that dog.

During my freshman year of high school they left me alone until I tried out for the football team. I made it to punching bag (third string); they made it to first string. I was covered in bruises all year. Each time a play was run, Bobby and Marco went out of their way to knock me into the dirt. I spent a lot of time thinking about Nina. How love hurts. How you pay for love with spilled food trays, stomped marbles, glued lockers, pink dogs, and blue bruises.

The summer before my junior year, my family and I moved to San Antonio. I went to a big school there, but through my cousins I made friends rather quickly. Whenever we went home to visit my grandmother, I'd try to catch a football game or two. I'd cheer every time Bobby or Marco was knocked to the ground. Nina was a cheerleader, and I loved watching her jump up and down when the team scored a touchdown—as long as it wasn't Bobby or Marco who had scored.

When I graduated, I attended the parties at both of my high schools, the one in San Antonio and the one in my hometown. I hadn't been home in about a year, and it was good to see everyone. Well, almost everyone. As I was pouring myself a cup of punch, I felt a hard hand fall on my right shoulder and then another hard hand fall on my left shoulder. I looked up. It was Bobby and Marco, and they were more gigantic than ever.

"How's it going, Luis?" Bobby asked with a grin.

"Yeah, vato, how's it going? Getting some punch and chocolate cake?" Marco said with an emphasis on *chocolate cake*.

I became nervous, but I tried to shake off my old bullies. After all, we were graduates now, not schoolboys. "Hey, guys, how you doing? Oh, you want some cake? Here, let me get out of your way."

I turned to make a fast exit, but there she was, coming toward us: Nina in a red satin dress. Bobby and Marco beamed with smiles and not enough innocence. I had thought I was over Nina. There were far prettier girls in San Antonio, and I'd even dated a few. But Nina was a girl from the Valley, sweeter than chocolate cake.

As she joined us, I tried to position myself as closely to

her as possible, but she chose to stand between Bobby and Marco. We all talked about our plans for the fall. I was going to college in San Antonio, and Bobby, Marco, and Nina planned to attend the local college. Bobby and Marco were being surprisingly nice to me, until I brought up Valentine's Day.

"Hey, remember the time in first grade," I said to Nina, "when these guys picked up your dress and you thought it was me?"

Nina looked confused, and the guys scowled and said, "Man, what are you talking about?"

I cleared my throat. "Yeah, remember? We were in first grade, in Ms. de los Santos's class, and you guys lifted up Nina's dress with your pencils." I turned to Nina. "And you thought it was me, but it was them. Remember?"

"What?" Nina said. "I know we were all in Ms. de los Santos's class, but I don't remember *that*." She looked at Bobby and Marco, and they shrugged.

I turned to the guys. "Remember? It was Valentine's Day. You two lifted Nina's dress, and I saw you do it. And I told Ms. de los Santos and I got your chocolate cake. Remember? I got your chocolate cake and you guys got nothing. Don't you remember?"

Nina began laughing. "Oh, Luis, you've always had an imagination."

"But it's true," I said.

"So what if it's true?" she answered. "Hello, that was elementary school. We're not little kids anymore. We're high school graduates now." And she walked off, shaking her head.

Once she was out of view, Bobby and Marco both turned to glare at me. They were the same glares I'd gotten before they knocked me off the monkey bars. They both let their heavy hands drop back on my shoulders, and they leaned toward me. Marco stuck his finger out and tapped my chest. "Hey, vato," he said, "why don't you have some chocolate cake for us? We haven't forgotten."

Papa Lalo

Harry's mouth dropped when his mother told him they were going to live with his grandfather Papa Lalo.

"What? I don't want to live with him. Can't we live with Grandfather Harold?"

"No. We're going to live with *our* family. In *our* home," she answered. Harry understood the implication: His father, Harold Bauer III, was no longer an acknowledged part of the family.

"But Papa Lalo is mean," Harry argued. "The man's a certified kitten killer."

His mother frowned. "What are you talking about?"

"Remember when I was six and my cat had kittens? Papa Lalo bashed each kitten's head against a tree and threw them in a plastic bag."

"Well, it's your father's fault for being so cheap that he wouldn't pay to get the cat fixed," Harry's mother said. "Besides, Papa Lalo took good care of that cat, got it fixed and everything."

"Yeah, until he ran over it with his truck," Harry said, throwing his arms up.

His mother sat down at the kitchen table and put her head in her hands. She looked up at him through watering eyes. Harry felt ashamed for thinking only about himself and making his mother cry.

"Mi'jo, I need your help, okay? You need to be strong and help me with your sisters. Papa Lalo wants us to live with him, and we can't stay here. I don't ever want to live here again, ever," she said through her breaking voice. "And besides, it stinks. I doubt the smell of smoke will ever come off these walls."

She was right. The house still reeked of smoke from the fire she'd set two weeks earlier. He couldn't blame her for what she'd done, pouring gas all over the master bedroom and setting it on fire. If Harry had caught his father with a man, he'd probably have done something drastic too.

She was admitted into a hospital so she could receive medication and counseling. The day after the fire Harry and his younger sisters, Stephanie and Michele, sat in the lobby of the hospital as Papa Lalo paced back and forth, grumbling in Spanish. Through all of his fourteen years Harry had been a little afraid of his Mexican grandfather, because the old man spoke only Spanish and did so in grumbles and grunts that even Harry's mother had trouble understanding. The only words Harry could pick up from Papa Lalo were *pinche gringo*. He knew then that he wouldn't be seeing his father anytime soon.

His mother gave Harry the job of telling his sisters that they'd be moving to Edcouch to live with Papa Lalo. They instantly began to whine.

"Can't we just stay with our friends like we've been doing?" Stephanie asked.

"Yeah, there isn't enough room in Papa Lalo's house," Michele added.

"Look, we're family and families stick together. Mom needs our help and we have to make some sacrifices," Harry said. "Besides, why would you want to stay here? The whole town is talking about us. I don't want to go to Edcouch either, but I don't want to stay *here*. So quit complaining, because whether you like it or not, we're leaving this stupid house." Stephanie and Michele straightened up and nodded.

The next day they packed what little had not been damaged by the fire. Papa Lalo drove up in his truck, stepped into the house, and put his arms out, grunting and mumbling.

"Why do I have to ride with him? I can't understand a word that man says," Harry complained under his breath to his mother as they packed boxes.

"He's not a man, he's your grandfather," she answered. "And he's speaking Spanish, your own language, so you better get used to it."

Harry rode with Papa Lalo in his truck. The old man turned the radio to his favorite Tejano station and sang along with some of the songs. Harry didn't know what was worse, the music or the old man's grunting.

Papa Lalo had a modest frame house with three small bedrooms, a kitchen, a garage that had been turned into a TV room with a washer and dryer, a living room that no one ever used, and a bathroom that didn't lock. Harry's sisters complained that the house was too small for all of them, but Harry's mother said that if her three brothers and two sisters could grow up in this house, they could too.

Every day Papa Lalo spent his late afternoons and early evenings at the Los Amigos sports bar. To Harry the house was calm only until his seventy-four-year-old grandfather came home at eight. His mother always saved a dinner plate for her father, who would take it outside to the backyard and sit in his green metal rocking chair, eating his dinner, smoking his Pall Mall cigarettes, and drinking beer. Next to his chair he had a radio, always turned up loud, and a small cooler that he filled with ice and a six-pack of beer. He'd listen to the Tejano music and tap his foot to the bajo sexto rhythms as he rocked back and forth.

Harry's room was the TV room, which had a big sofa and a window air-conditioning unit. Even over the rumble of the air conditioner he could usually hear the old man grunting and grumbling along with the songs on the radio, but he'd just turn up the volume on the TV. At nine o'clock sharp, the old man would walk in and take the remote con-

trol, automatically changing the channel to a Spanish program, no matter what anyone else was watching.

No one in the family questioned Papa Lalo. Harry's
mother and sisters would go to their rooms, where they had
their own little TVs. Harry would have liked to go outside,
but he couldn't stand the night heat like the old man could,
so he was forced to stay in the air-conditioned room and
watch the Spanish programs with his grandfather.

Papa Lalo switched between the three Spanish channels:
one with boxing or soccer, the second with game shows in
which women in short dresses ran around, and the last with
nothing but telenovelas.

Telenovelas were the old man's favorite. Harry shook his
head in disbelief at his grandfather's ability to watch over-
acted soap operas until eleven o'clock every night. Harry
counted the days until he could go to Boy Scout camp for
two weeks. The year before, Harry had hated camp, but
TV night after TV night, it was starting to sound good.

Papa Lalo tried to get the boy involved in his favorite
telenovelas by offering him Cracker Jack that he ate out of
a bowl. But Harry would politely say no in his best Spanish.
The old man often interacted with his programs, grunting
or laughing at the action on the TV. Sometimes he would
give a shout of triumph and clap his hands when some
double-crossed wife slapped a man or ran him out of her
house.

At times the grandfather looked over to his grandson or
gave him a nudge when the adulterer was caught red-

handed or when the soap opera family stepped in to rescue a troubled daughter or son. The old man would nod and grunt with conviction, and Harry would do the same, then roll his eyes as soon as Papa Lalo turned back to the TV.

One night at 8:58 P.M. Harry's mother and sisters walked out of the TV room as usual to make way for Papa Lalo. Harry, now resigned to the routine, changed the channel to his grandfather's favorite telenovela, but the old man didn't come in. At 9:02 there was still no sign of Papa Lalo. Harry got up, opened the back door, and stuck his head out. The old man was still, his body slumped to one side and his head turned down at an angle. There was no foot-tapping, no rocking, and no singing.

Harry imagined himself explaining to his mother and sisters how he had found Papa Lalo dead. How he'd had nothing to do with it. He hadn't even touched him. Nothing. He'd just found him like that. Dead. Honest.

Harry reached out and shook the old man's shoulder gently and then a little harder. He whispered his name so he would not wake him if he were dead. But the old man's eyes sparked open and he grunted. He looked at his watch and stood up, grumbling. Harry moved to one side to let the man pass; Papa Lalo was now in a rush so as not to miss one more bad dramatic pause from his leading lady.

During a commercial break the old man stepped outside, then came back in with two beers and gave one to Harry. He gestured for Harry to drink, and the boy said in English, "Are you going to tell my mother?"

Papa Lalo laughed and said in clear Spanish, "Yo soy el hombre de la casa." He toasted his grandson, and the two *men* drank their beer and ate Cracker Jack.

Once a week Harry's mother drove him to Harlingen so he could attend his Boy Scout meetings. At one of the meetings a fellow Scout brought two rabbits to give away: a white one with pink eyes and a gray one with brown eyes. The Scouts petted the rabbits and let them run around the hall as they discussed their upcoming camping trip. When Harry's mother returned to pick him up, Harry persuaded her to ask Papa Lalo if he could keep the rabbits. After all, there was a big empty cage in the backyard, and they did live in the country. His mother called Papa Lalo on her cell phone, then reported that he had given his okay even though he'd said that "rabbits are for eating."

Harry fed the rabbits twice a day and even made leashes out of twine so they could walk around the backyard. His grandfather sometimes sat in his green chair, smoking, frowning at the rabbits as they nibbled on the grass, and grumbling to himself.

The day before Harry left for camp, he laid out all his equipment and clothes on the floor of the TV room. He went over his checklist to make sure he had everything he needed: cooking kit, knife, compass, flashlight, socks, underwear, first-aid kit, canteen, T-shirts, sunblock, hat, Boy Scout handbook, snakebite kit, insect repellent, toothbrush, floss, toilet paper. The old man grunted as he watched the boy check off the items. He walked out of the room and then came back in, holding a small brown leather case. He held the case out to Harry and motioned for the boy to take it.

Harry held the case, and Papa Lalo grumbled for him to open it. Inside was a sparkling stainless steel object, but Harry couldn't tell what it was. He took it out of the case and looked at it, but the old man kept gesturing at him. Harry didn't know what he was trying to say.

Finally Papa Lalo took the object from the boy and demonstrated. He flipped a latch to the side and opened the stainless steel octagon as if he were showing a jewel. It was a compass. A surveyor's compass. Not plastic like Harry's Boy Scout compass, but a real one. Papa Lalo had worked for the highway department for thirty years, clearing land and building roads all across south Texas. The compass had been a tool left from those years of hard work.

Thick glass covered the north, south, east, and west indicators, surrounded by polished stainless steel. Mathematical formulas that would take Harry years to understand were engraved on the back, along with his grandfather's name, Eduardo Salinas Cuéllar. The old man handed the compass to his grandson and smiled, then walked outside to sit in his chair. Harry turned to the compass-reading chapter in his Boy Scout handbook as Tejano music from his grandfather's radio pushed aside the hot evening.

Harry and his mother were running late the next morning. By the time they arrived in Harlingen to meet the Boy Scout troop, all the other Scouts had finished loading the vans with their backpacks and tents. Harry was the last one.

His mother wanted to hug him, but he frowned. "Mom, I'm fourteen now. Pop the trunk—I gotta go. They're waiting for me." He grabbed his backpack out of the trunk and rushed to the waiting vans.

It wasn't until the Boy Scouts were on the road that Harry realized he'd forgotten to tell his mother to feed his rabbits. "Your grandfather will feed them," his friend said to reassure him, but Harry just looked out the window and answered, "Oh, yeah, he'll feed them all right—enough to fatten them up so he can eat them."

Camp was good for Harry. He was so happy to be away from his family's problems that two weeks felt too short. He hardly thought about his father and about Papa Lalo, and he wondered about his rabbits only once or twice.

The last night of camp Harry took an inventory of his equipment. He went through his checklist of belongings while his tentmate watched, and the boy couldn't resist grabbing the brown leather compass case.

"What's in this? Can I look?" he asked.

"Go ahead, but don't drop it," Harry said.

The boy took out the shiny object and marveled, "Wow, what is this?"

"It's my compass," Harry said. "My grandfather gave it to me."

"Cool. How do you open it?" he asked.

"There's a little latch on the side. Here, let me show you." Harry took the compass and flipped it open. "See, it's easy. Just gotta know how to do it."

"Your grandfather *gave* you this?" the boy asked as he studied the compass. "My grandfather doesn't let me near his stuff. Yours must be pretty cool."

Harry shrugged his shoulders. "Yeah, when I think about it, I guess he is."

The minute Harry returned to his grandfather's house, he dropped his equipment in the TV room and rushed out to the rabbit cage. But the rabbits weren't there. The cage was completely empty—no bowls of water, no hay, nothing. He looked around the backyard, hoping that by some miracle they'd be hopping around. They weren't. He looked through the flower garden, but they weren't there either. And then he saw them: two rabbit hides, one white and one gray, nailed to the wall of his grandfather's shed.

Harry screamed at the top of his lungs for all the dead animals of the world to hear. "That man killed my rabbits! What the hell is wrong with him?"

Harry's mother came rushing out of the house, but Harry didn't wait to hear what she had to say. He jumped on his mountain bike and started racing to town, still dressed in his full Boy Scout uniform. There was only one place the old man could be: Los Amigos sports bar. Harry made the one-mile trip in record time, cursing his grandfather the whole way.

Sure enough, Papa Lalo's faded yellow truck was parked in front of the sports bar. Harry pulled the door open and walked in, ignoring the sign that read NO ONE UNDER 21 AL-

LOWED. There was his grandfather, grunting and grumbling at a pool table with some skinny man Harry didn't know.

Harry stomped over to his grandfather with his fists clenched, and through his breaking voice he said, "You killed my rabbits, didn't you?" The old man grumbled an answer, using hand gestures to try to explain how no one had been feeding the rabbits, how they were almost dead as it was. They had been suffering, the old man seemed to be saying. But Harry didn't want to understand. "I hate you, I hate you!" he shouted, and he ran out crying.

The old man followed him and reached into his pocket for a rabbit's foot he had saved. He held it out and grunted for the boy to wait. "Those rabbits were almost dead," he muttered. "They were suffering." But Harry just got back on his bike and rode home in tears.

Harry buried the rabbit pelts in the flower garden and said as little as possible to his grandfather after that, though the old man tried. While watching his telenovelas, Papa Lalo pointed out scene after scene of forgiveness in the dramas, managing only to annoy his grandson. It may have been this annoyance that finally led Harry to abandon his grudge. One day during a dramatic pause by one of the characters, the boy threw up his arms and said okay. The old man smiled and offered his grandson some Cracker Jack.

By August Harry and his sisters were enrolled at the Edcouch-Elsa Independent School District. Harry tried to persuade his mother to let him live with his friends in Harlingen and go to school there. But his mother said if Edcouch-Elsa High School was good enough for her, then it was good enough for him.

After the first day of school word spread from girl to girl that Harry was cute and didn't have a girlfriend, and within a month he was asked to be an escort for a quinceañera. He wanted to say no, but the girl had a desperate look, as though Harry were her last hope. And he was. Somebody told him that the girl's boyfriend was still up north in the fields and that none of the other guys she'd asked could afford to rent a tux. So Harry reluctantly asked his mother if she would pay for the rental. She smiled gleefully and said, "We always have money for a dance!"

Harry and his family went to the mall in McAllen to rent his tuxedo. His sisters did their own shopping while his mother and Papa Lalo escorted Harry to Antonio's Man Shop. The store attendant took the boy's measurements, then had him try on some coats. The first one was too big, which made Papa Lalo chuckle. Harry rolled his eyes, and his mother swatted him on the arm.

The night of the quinceañera Harry took a good shower and dressed in his mother's room. As he put on his coat, he found thirty dollars in the inside pocket. Lucky day, he thought. Standing in front of his mother's full-length mirror, he smiled at his reflection. He thought he looked pretty cool.

When he walked into the kitchen in his rented shoes and tuxedo, his sisters and mother oohed and ahhed. His mother gave him a corsage for his date and said, "You are such a handsome young man."

Papa Lalo agreed. "Mira qué chulo yo," he said in a gruff but clear voice.

Harry threw up his arms. "Okay, enough already. Let's go."

During the drive to the Coyote Dance Hall Harry showed his mother the money he'd found. "I think somebody forgot it," he said.

"Harry, people don't forget money. Your grandfather put it there."

"Why did he do that?" Harry asked.

His mother smiled. "Because he was young once and your grandmother loved to dance."

After Harry's third quinceañera in less than two months, Papa Lalo said why not just buy a tuxedo. The attendant at Antonio's Man Shop gave Harry a wink as he handed him a gold plastic garment bag imprinted with the store logo, Don Quixote on a horse.

"I included a hundred-percent cotton French-cuff shirt and gold-plated cuff links," he said with a smile. "I knew you were going to buy it." He gave Harry a discount and threw in a pair of black socks.

With every quinceañera Harry's mother and sisters had the same reaction: oohs and ahhs. Papa Lalo would always let out a grito and say, "Mira qué chulo yo." And Harry always found some spending cash in his coat pocket. It became a routine, but he couldn't help blushing each time his papa Lalo called him chulo.

At one of the quinceañeras Harry's grandfather was the padrino of the music. The whole family dressed up and attended together, Harry in his tuxedo, his mother and sisters in dresses, and his grandfather in a shiny black Western-cut suit with black cowboy boots and a black cowboy hat. When the old man stepped out of his room in full garb, he wiggled his hips mischievously and smiled a smile straight from a Pall Mall ad.

Harry watched as his grandfather danced to almost every song. If his mother or sisters weren't free, Papa Lalo danced with any woman he could find. He twirled them around the dance floor as if he were half his age. And when Harry himself danced, Papa Lalo would clap and shout, "Este es mi hijo!"

Men kept coming up to Harry's grandfather to shake his hand as if he were the county judge, and Papa Lalo proudly introduced his family each time. Putting his arm around Harry he'd say, "Este es mi hijo Harry," and Harry was surprised to find that he liked these introductions. He even secretly liked the fact that his mother made him pose for a picture with Papa Lalo.

By February Papa Lalo's house had grown to feel like home. Toward the end of the month Harry and his grandfather spent a busy Saturday doing yard work together. They cut the grass and repainted the tree trunks white.

They removed hanging limbs and piled them up for a fire later. They planted new flowers in the garden and pulled weeds. They washed both cars.

For dinner the family ate fajitas that Papa Lalo had grilled outside, and rice and beans made by Harry's mother. Harry sat outside in the backyard with his grandfather afterward and demonstrated his talent for knocking over empty beer cans with his blowgun. The old man tried to blow a bead through the blowgun, but could manage only a farting sound. They both laughed.

At 8:55 P.M. Harry's mother and sisters cleared out of the TV room, and Harry changed the channel to his grandfather's telenovela. Right at 9:00 Harry called out to his grandfather, but there was no reply. Harry got up to wake the old man. Papa Lalo's head was to one side and his hand still held his beer loosely. Harry laughed to himself and gently tapped Papa Lalo on the shoulder. But the old man did not respond. Harry tapped his shoulder once more and spoke his name.

"Papa Lalo, your show is on," he said. But the old man didn't open his eyes. It was then that Harry realized Papa Lalo looked different. Harry could feel his heart speeding and he called out again.

"Papa Lalo, Papa . . . you need to wake up!" He shook the man. "Papa, get up!" He backed up and shouted through the screen door, "Mom! Grandfather isn't waking up!"

Harry took his grandfather gently in his arms and laid him on the wooden patio. Scanning his mind for the first-aid techniques he'd learned at Boy Scout camp, he began mouth to mouth. His mother came to the door and he screamed, "Call 911." Harry pressed his lips against his grandfather's and pushed his own breath into the old man's chest. He didn't stop until the ambulance arrived. He was covered in sweat when they took Papa Lalo away.

The next morning the phone didn't stop ringing, and relatives Harry didn't know kept coming over and not leaving. Harry stayed outside even though they all wanted to meet the brave boy. He thought for a long while and then went inside to his grandfather's room, where he opened the closet and stared at the old man's black suit.

Later that afternoon his mother searched the closet for the suit, but she couldn't find it. She searched all the closets and began to cry. Harry's sisters tried to help, but they couldn't find it either. Harry sat outside in his grandfather's green chair, overhearing the conversation. Where could the suit be? It was here yesterday. Maybe he took it to the cleaners? Lent it to somebody? Gave it away?

Harry went inside. "Why don't you just put him in my tux?" he said. "It's black."

"We can't put him in a tuxedo. He's not going to a dance," his mother answered.

"He liked the tuxedo," Harry argued.

"And what if you get invited to another quinceañera?"

"I don't feel like dancing."

"No, Harry, you need that tuxedo," his mother said.

"I want Papa Lalo to have it. Please!" Harry's eyes began to water and his face reddened. "I want him to wear it. He would like it."

Harry's mother hugged him. She brushed his hair back and he held her tight. "Please, Mom," he said. "Let him wear my tuxedo."

At the rosary people whispered that they wouldn't be surprised if at any minute Papa Lalo awakened—ready to dance. His gray hair and moustache were groomed to perfection, the hair gel reflecting a glimmer of fluorescent light. There was a hint of blush on his cheeks as if Papa Lalo were a little chiflado in his tux, and light powder softened his face, making him look young again. His fingers seemed to caress the satin lapels of his jacket. The gold-plated cuff links sparkled and his bow tie was perfectly knotted. The guests found it difficult not to touch him.

Sitting outside in the green chair a few nights later, Harry gently rocked as he passed his grandfather's compass between his hands. He looked out over the garden at the dark pile of dead branches. In his back pocket was a box of matches. He stood up and placed the compass on the chair, then walked into his grandfather's shed. He walked out with a gallon container of gasoline, poured it over the branches, struck a match, and tossed it onto the pile.

The flames grew with the Valley breeze, and Harry watched them until he felt the heat on his face. Then he went back inside the shed and came out with Papa Lalo's black suit. He threw it onto the fire, and the flames grabbed it instantly. He sat back down on the metal chair to watch the fire. The compass in his hand shined orange and red, and when he turned it over, the letters of his grandfather's name glowed in the dark.

Crazy Loco

On my eighth birthday my brother and I got the puppy we had begged for. He was part German shepherd and part something else that was very fluffy. We didn't call him Fluffy, though. We wanted to, but there was some other dog in our neighborhood named Fluffy.

Our dog didn't have a name for two weeks. We couldn't decide what to call him. Dad said we had to wait for the puppy to do something unusual, and then we could give him a name that fit what he had done.

We watched him carefully. One day he followed our cat, Kitty Meow Meow, into a brown bag and couldn't get out, so we tried naming him Losty, Baggy, and Kitty. But when we called him Losty, he looked as if he were frowning. And when we called him Baggy and Kitty, his ears didn't move.

He fell a lot, so we tried Stumbles, but that was a dumb name. He liked to roll around, so we thought of Rolly. But we had a cousin named Rolly, so we couldn't call him that.

He liked to chew on everything, so we wanted to call him Chewy, but we also had a cousin named Chuy. Though he had brown fur, we couldn't call our puppy Brownie, because there were two dogs in our neighborhood named Brownie. He liked to bark a lot, but Barky was just as dumb a name as Stumbles. He liked to lick caca, but we would never name him that.

In frustration my brother and I decided one morning to just start calling out names: Lassie, Rin Tin Tin, Lucky, Pepe, Pongo, Rex, Chile, Pepper, Rover, Sparky, King, Killer, Max, Rocky, Spot (though the dog had no spots), Bonita (but we had a cousin named Bonita, and besides, our dog was a boy), Chulo, Wolf, Perro, Corvette, Trans Am, Ferrari, Rooster, Tiger, Elephant, Snake, Cobra, Lizard, Shark, Fire, Eagle, Devil Dog, Hot Dog, Enchilada, Taco, Burrito, Nacho (n'hombre, no—we had a cousin named Nacho too), Chalupa, Chorizo, Fajita, Tortilla, Queso. Our dog didn't respond to any of the names we used.

That's when our father walked in. We told him what we were doing and he decided to try. "Lobo," he started. "Fido, Rex, Blackie, Fluffy." We told Dad we had used those names, but he kept on. "Speedy Gonzales, Slow Poke Rodríguez, Coyote, Bugs Bunny, Road Runner, Yosemite Sam, Tasmanian Devil, Cantinflas, El Chavo del Ocho, El Chapulín Colorado, Mil Máscaras, Perro Sonso!" But nothing worked. Our dog just chomped on his chew bone and growled.

The following week we were all getting into our car to go shopping in McAllen when our nameless dog jumped into the driver's seat. My father took him out, and as soon as he plunked him down on the ground, the dog ran right back into the car. "Perro sonso, get out of the car," Dad said. But the dog just barked and put his front paws on top of the steering wheel.

My mother shook her head and said, "Qué *loco* está este perro!" And that's how our dog, Loco, got his name.

From then on Loco took many rides with us in the car. He always wanted to get in the front seat with our parents, but Mom wouldn't let him. We'd take him grocery shopping and to visit our cousins. If we left him in the car by himself, we'd roll all the windows down so Loco wouldn't get hot. When we returned, we always found him with his front paws on the steering wheel, ready to drive away.

He followed my brother and me all over town as we rode our bikes, always taking his time to smell things and pee on plants, cars, and trucks. If we called him, he'd catch up to us fast but then pass us to smell and pee on more things. Whenever we rode out to the canals, Loco jumped in the water and started barking. We'd ride along the canal and he'd swim beside us, barking as loudly as he could. Nobody else in town had a dog that could swim.

One Saturday we went to the local swimming pool and Loco managed to sneak in behind us. When he saw the water, he ran and jumped in before we could stop him. All the kids in the pool started screaming, and the lifeguards tried to get Loco out with a long hook. But he was too fast for them. He kept barking and swimming out of reach. The lifeguards made the kids get out of the pool. Then one of them had to dive in and carry Loco out.

When the lifeguard set him down by the side of the pool, Loco shook his moplike body, then jumped right back in, barking even louder. I think he was bark-laughing.

All the kids were laughing too, as were some of the grown-ups. Two lifeguards jumped in and caught Loco again, but this time they didn't set him down until he was outside the pool gate. My brother and I had to take Loco home, and our friends told us that it took almost an hour for the lifeguards to get all of Loco's hair out of the pool with their nets.

We were afraid that our parents would be mad when we told them what Loco had done, but they laughed and Loco started barking. I guess Loco thought it was funny too. That summer our parents bought us a plastic swimming pool, but it was really for Loco.

Loco's other favorite pastime was chasing things. He chased everything—except cars, which just goes to show that he wasn't that loco after all. He chased flies, birds, balls, sapos . . . everything. All the cats in the neighborhood were afraid of him. Not Kitty Meow Meow, though. Loco would open his mouth and put the cat's whole head inside and just carry him around the yard. It didn't seem to bother Kitty Meow Meow at all.

Loco even loved chasing cuetes. We'd light one and throw it, and Loco would race over to sniff it. We'd yell,

"You crazy dog! Can't you see the fuse is lit?" We'd try to keep him away from the firecracker, but he'd always run right back to it and put his nose inches from the sparkling fuse. Then, palo! Loco would jump back and start barking, his nose singed.

He'd chase bottle rockets too. We'd put one in a bottle and light it, and when it fired up into the sky, Loco would jump up and down, trying to catch it. When the bottle rocket went pop in the sky, he'd run around in circles, barking ecstatically. The only problem was that sometimes he'd knock over the bottle before it fired, and then we'd scream and dash away, hoping the rocket wouldn't come toward us and blow up. Our friends said we should just tie up Loco, but my brother and I thought that would take all the fun out of it.

One day we were in the monte by our house, sitting around eating our Hunt's Snack-Pack Pudding, when Loco got up from his sleeping position and began sniffing the air. Before we could even blink, there went Loco, running and barking after a possum. But clumsy Loco was in such a rush that he ran straight into some nopales!

Eeeeeeloooo! We sucked in our breath at the sight of Loco's left shoulder. It was covered with espinas. But Loco refused to whine as we walked him home, and he limped only a little.

When we got home, our mother pulled out the espinas one by one, using tweezers and rubbing alcohol. My brother and I cringed each time she pulled one out, but Loco didn't make a sound. He just sat next to Mom on the porch, every now and then turning to lick her hand as she worked.

"See how brave Loco is?" Mom said to us. "Last time I pulled espinas out of you two, you cried like a couple of babies. You should be more like Loco."

"Like what?" my brother said. "You mean we should try to eat a cuete?" He and I laughed.

"Huercos sonsos," our mother muttered as she pulled out another espina.

Loco didn't sleep in the house like Kitty Meow Meow did. He slept outside and sometimes at night he barked, especially if the town siren rang out its fire alert. When the siren called members of the Edcouch Volunteer Fire Department out of their beds, all the dogs in the neighborhood barked their own alerts. Loco's bark was always the loudest. But one night the siren went off and Loco didn't make a sound. Our father was one of the volunteer firemen, and when he came back from the grass fire that night, he told us that Loco was nowhere to be found.

The next day my brother and I rode our bikes around town looking for him. We rode out to the canal, but he wasn't there. We rode to the town swimming pool, but he wasn't there either. We rode to the monte and called out his name over and over again, but there was no answer. For two days no Loco. Then on the third day, there he was on the front porch, seeming as happy to see us as we were to see him. And it wasn't the last time he was to disappear. For the next

year Loco was gone at least once a month. Where he went
was a real mystery. Dad said Loco had a girlfriend in Elsa,
the town next to Edcouch, but my brother and I didn't think
Loco was good-looking enough to have a girlfriend.

It was a Saturday afternoon when Loco did his final dis-
appearing act. The whole family was going shopping in
McAllen. Loco jumped into the car with us as usual, but
Mom and Dad said we couldn't take him because we'd be
out all day. Dad dragged Loco out of the car, but the dog
just hopped right back into the driver's seat and put his
front paws on the steering wheel. He barked and went
"grrrrrrrrr"—but in a nice way.

"Come on, Mom and Dad, let Loco come with us," my
brother and I pleaded. Dad started to say that Loco shouldn't
stay in the car all day long, but Loco *loved* being in the car,
and we all knew it.

The summer before, we'd taken a family trip all the way
to Madera, California, to visit our tía and tío and all our
cousins. We had taken Loco in the car with us. He sat in
back with a big bag of dog food and a water bowl that spilled
every time the road got bumpy. It was a great vacation. Our
cousins had a dog named Trixie; we told Loco that Trixie
was his cousin, and they got along great. Trixie liked swimming too. When we went to the lake near our cousin's house,
Loco and Trixie were the first ones in the water. Loco
whimpered for a whole week after we left California.

So whenever Mom and Dad said we couldn't take Loco
in the car with us, we always argued, "If he can go all the

way to California, he can go anywhere!" This particular time Loco gave a loud bark, as if he were saying yes. And Mom and Dad couldn't help but give in.

When we got to the mall in McAllen, we parked the car on the shady side of the lot, left Loco a big bowl of water and a dog biscuit, and rolled all the windows down just enough for him to be able to stick his head out. Loco barked happily after us as we walked away.

We shopped for a couple of hours, and then my brother and I wanted to go back to the car to let Loco out for a walk. Our parents decided that it was time to go home anyway, so we all walked back to the shady side of the parking lot. But our car was gone.

Mom and Dad started wondering out loud, "Did we park somewhere else? Could the car have been towed away?" But they were forgetting the most important question.

"What about Loco?" my brother and I yelled.

Our parents quickly tried to reassure us that Loco was fine. "He's a smart dog," Dad said as he patted his thighs. "Wait a minute. I think I left the keys in the car!" He searched his pockets and then asked Mom if she had them.

"You were the one driving," she said.

My brother began to cry. "Someone stole our car—and Loco too!"

Mom gave my brother a hug. "Mi'jito, don't worry. I'm sure Loco is okay. Mira, let's all go inside and call the police. Maybe they already know where the car is."

We went back inside the mall and alerted the police, and

Dad called our tío in Weslaco to loan us a car. All the way home my brother cried, but Mom and Dad kept saying that we should think positive and that the police would do the best they could to find Loco.

That same afternoon Mom made a lost-dog flier with Loco's photo on it. It was a picture we had taken during our drive to California. Mom made lots of copies of the flier, and we put them up all over the mall and in the neighborhood nearby. We even went to the dog pound in McAllen to look for Loco, but he wasn't one of the sad dogs there. At that point my brother and I both cried a little bit. We gave the pound one of our fliers in case Loco showed up later.

For two weeks no one called, and our parents got a check from the insurance company, because they said the car was most likely stolen. A couple of days later we went into McAllen to shop for a new car, and Mom and Dad took us back to the dog pound to check for Loco one last time. He still wasn't there, but the woman behind the counter said we could adopt one of their dogs if we wanted to.

My brother looked at our mother and said, "Mom, can we?"

The woman behind the counter said, "We have a dog that looks a lot like Loco, and he can catch Frisbees too."

Mom shrugged. "Well, you guys want to look at him?"

We both shouted yes and followed the woman into the room with all the dog cages. A fluffy brown dog jumped up and began to bark at us in a friendly way. "One of the guys who works here named him Sparky," the woman told us, "but if you want him, you can call him anything you like."

My brother put his hands up to the metal cage and the dog licked them. Then my father and I put our hands up to the cage, and Sparky barked, then licked us too. "I think he likes us," Mom said.

And that's how Sparky became our second dog. Mom and Dad paid the adoption fee, and we walked out of the pound with a new pet. Sparky jumped right into the car just like Loco used to.

My brother rode in the backseat with Sparky, and I got in the front with Mom and Dad. There was a lost-Loco flier on the floor, and I picked it up to look at the picture of Loco. He was in the driver's seat with his paws on the steering wheel and his tongue sticking out. He looked so happy in our old car.

"Mom, where do you think Loco is?" I asked.

"You know what? I think since we left the keys in the car, Loco turned it on and drove away. And I'll bet you he's in California somewhere."

I smiled. "You think so?"

"Oh, yeah," Mom said. "Loco wasn't a dumb dog, just a crazy one."

Proud to Be an American

Every time my family and I came back across the border after shopping in Las Flores for good lecha quemada, or getting a haircut, or buying pills for my grandmother, a border patrolman would stop our car. He'd place his hand on the roof, lean forward, and ask us, in a Texas cowboy accent, "Y'all American citizens?"

Dad would answer proudly, "Yes, sir," and then turn to us kids with a big smile and say, "Richard, Paul, Steven, tell the nice man, 'Yes, sir.'" We'd repeat the phrase in unison, nodding vigorously. And as we crossed the checkpoint, Dad would always give the patrolman a quick salute.

Dad was proud to be an American and to have served his country bravely in Vietnam, just like my tío Paco and tío Javier. They all got drafted in '68. Tío Javier didn't come back. When I was born in 1969, Mom and Dad named me after President Richard Nixon because they hoped one day I'd be president.

Dad liked the army so much that when he came back, he joined the National Guard. Tío Paco tried to join too, but was put in some hospital after he reacted badly to a machine-gun exercise. He seemed to go to the hospital a lot. I remember visiting him there once. He gave me a box he'd made out of wood and painted with a peace sign and flowers. I used the flower box to keep the BBs for my BB gun.

Often Dad would take my brothers and me to the National Guard armory when he had to report for duty. We'd get to play in jeeps and sometimes on tanks and hang by the muzzle barrel. We'd beg Dad to let us inside the tanks, but he didn't think his commanding officer would allow it. To us the armory was like a big gym. It even had basketball nets, and we'd play basketball while Dad drank beer with his army buddies and waited for four o'clock to come around.

Every time Dad went away to a fort with the Guard, he'd bring home boxes of army food, and it was the best! Everything came in green packages: beef slices, spaghetti and meatballs, fruit cocktail, and chocolate bars (which were called John Wayne bars).

Our maid, Rosie, didn't approve of the army food. She'd frown at us while we sat in the kitchen eating from our green cans. "That food has no taste," she'd say as she cooked rice and beans at the stove.

"It's American food," one of us would answer.

"Well, it has no flavor. It's boring," Rosie would say with a flick of her spoon. "I don't know how you boys can stand the stuff. Your dog eats better."

But we loved everything Dad brought home from his Guard duty. Our home was filled with army items. We had army lightbulbs, motor oil, batteries, a hammer, sleeping bags, canteens, a flashlight, rain ponchos, blankets, and even army toilet paper. Everything was painted green, except the toilet paper. And our very favorite thing Dad brought home were blanks of M-16 bullets.

Most of the time the brass blanks were empty and tarnished from having been fired at some unknown enemy. Once when I was ten we asked Rosie for the Brasso she used to polish Dad's belt and buttons.

"What do you want it for?" she asked.

"We're going to polish these bullets," my brother Steven said, showing them to her.

Rosie took a blank bullet in her hand and studied it. "Where did you get these?" she asked, her brow furrowed.

"They're army bullets. We got them from our father," my other brother, Paul, said with pride.

Rosie shook her head and got us the Brasso and an old T-shirt. "Here. Go outside to clean them and don't get your clothes dirty."

That was the first of many times we borrowed the Brasso from Rosie. We'd shine our bullets until they looked like tiny bars of gold, then stand them up in rows on our porch and try to shoot them off with our BB guns. And occasionally we'd find some that still had bullet powder in them. For those we had a different game.

Inside the top of the blanks was a little red cap that held

the powder in place. All we had to do was punch a hole in the cap with a nail and all the powder would pour out. The powder looked like tiny silver beans, and it was better than a whole box of John Wayne bars. We'd pour it on an ant and strike a match. There'd be a white flash and the ant would be toast. But there was never enough bullet powder to have real fun. Then one day, while going through Dad's green army trunk, we found a metal case that contained hundreds of M-60 blanks.

The M-60 blanks were bigger and had more powder than M-16 bullets. Paul and I thought about covering the whole anthill with a layer of powder and burning all the ants at once, but Steven had the best idea ever. "Let's make a grenade," he said. We shouted with excitement and rushed into the kitchen to find a tin can.

The perfect can, quart size, was in the refrigerator, still half full of grapefruit juice. We drank the rest of the juice, removed the top with the can opener, and were happily drying the can when Rosie entered the kitchen.

Seeing us working together instead of fighting, she became suspicious. "What are you kids up to?" she asked with her brow raised.

"We're making a bomba!" Steven shouted gleefully.

Rosie closed her eyes and sighed. "What for?"

"To blow up on the Fourth of July," Steven announced. This was news to Paul and me, but we instantly approved.

"Ah, sí, you like the Fourth of July?" Rosie asked.

"Yeah," I said. "We get to set off firecrackers and chase Dad's big army flare!"

Every Fourth of July Dad brought home an army flare, a silver cylinder that looked like three Pillsbury biscuit cans stacked on top of one another. It was better than the biggest Roman candle we could buy. Dad would stand in the middle of the street and fire off the flare into the Valley night. A white streak would zoom into the air, the light so bright that it turned the night into day. We'd jump on our bikes and chase the floating light, shouting, "Happy Fourth of July" to anyone we passed.

Rosie frowned but nodded at our grenade plan. "I'll watch you build this *bomba*," she said. She followed us outside and sat at the edge of our back porch, drinking a glass of water as we worked.

When we'd emptied all the blanks into the tin can, we had filled only half of it, so we decided to use two Coke cans instead. We would test one on the anthill and save the other one for the Fourth of July.

We filled up the Coke cans with powder, covered the drinking holes with duct tape, and then smashed the cans with a cinder block to pack them tight so they'd explode real well. Then we punched one small hole in each can, stuck fuses inside, and poured a little more powder around the fuses. At each step of the process we looked up at Rosie, and she shook her head and mumbled something in Spanish.

Once the grenades were all set we walked over to the anthill and placed one on top of the hole so the ants would crawl all over it. We told Rosie to go inside just in case it was a big explosion. She rolled her eyes but went in and stood at the screen door to watch. When the bomba was fully covered with ants, we lit the fuse and ran behind the garage, covering our ears. But the bomba didn't explode. Instead it started smoking and making a hissing sound. Sparks shot out of the drinking hole that was covered with the tape, and the can started to melt. Rosie burst out laughing.

My brothers and I cautiously walked over to the burning can. "Why didn't it blow up?" Paul said. "It should have blown up."

"What are we going to do?" Steven said. "Tomorrow is the Fourth of July."

"Maybe we should have used a bottle," I said. I held the second can in my hands and studied it, then walked over to Rosie.

"Do you have a jar with a lid or a Coke bottle we can use?" I asked her through the screen door.

"Ya no. Give me that can before you burn yourselves." She opened the door and snatched the can from my hand. "When your parents come home from work, you can have it back."

"It's supposed to be a surprise," I said. But Rosie had already walked away. For the rest of the afternoon we tried our best to get back our grenade, but Rosie wouldn't budge.

When she told our father about it that evening, he was pretty mad. But as soon as we said it was for the Fourth of July, he broke into a proud smile.

"Yeah, Dad, it'd be like a big firecracker," Paul said.

"Yeah, Dad," Steven added. "We weren't going to hurt anything—just blow it up."

"Well, we won't need your *bomba* tomorrow night," Dad said, "because I have a surprise for you guys."

"Are you still going to bring the flare?" Paul asked.

"Yes, and also something extra special. But you have to promise me something." We all nodded. "You cannot go through my army trunk anymore. That's U.S. government property and we have to respect that. Okay?"

"We promise," the three of us said solemnly.

The next day we put out the American flag on the front porch, and Mom and Dad went grocery shopping for our annual Fourth of July barbecue. At five o'clock Dad started a fire in the barbecue pit for fajitas and chicken. Rosie and Mom cooked rice and beans, and Paul cut open the avocados to make dip. We always fought over the avocados, because whoever cut them open got to keep the pits for his slingshot.

While the fajitas cooked, Dad took us to the Mr. Bang firework stand off of Highway 107. The man who owned it was Mr. Benavides, but everyone called him Sergeant B; he was the head National Guard supply sergeant for the whole Valley. Dad and Sergeant B exchanged handshakes and talked while we kids told his wife, who worked in the stand with him, what we wanted. Dad and the sergeant walked around to the back of the stand, and Dad came back with a brown bag. Sergeant B gave us a discount, and we drove home happy. We kept asking Dad what was in the bag, but he said we'd have to wait and see.

When we got home, Mom and Rosie had the food ready, and we all sat outside on the porch eating from army paper plates. Dad always saved the flare until ten, so in the meantime we set off our firecrackers, bottle rockets, Roman candles, twisters, smoke bombs, and sparklers. The sparklers were for Mom. She liked to make figure eights and zigzag lines with the fizzing sticks. Rosie was afraid of burning herself, but Mom taught her how to hold one, and she started making designs in the air too. My brothers and I thought the sparklers were boring because they didn't blow up.

We kept a close eye on our watches, and at ten we began chanting, "Flare, flare, flare, flare."

Dad stood up and put out his hands. "Okay, okay. Everyone stay here. I'll be right back," he said.

"Are you going to get the surprise?" Steven asked.

"Just wait right here," Dad said, smiling.

He went into the house and came back with the brown bag. We all stood up in anticipation—except Mom and Rosie, who stayed seated. Dad reached into the bag with a devil grin on his face and pulled out a white container the size of a soda can.

"Is that a small flare?" Mom asked.

Dad shook his head. "Nope, it's a grenade simulator!"

All our mouths dropped, and my brothers and I started jumping up and down.

"Can we hold it?" we all asked.

"When you join the army, you can hold it."

"Wait a second," Mom said. "Kids, get away from that thing. What are you going to do with that?" She did not look happy.

"We're going to set it off to celebrate the Fourth of July," Dad said. "And then we'll shoot the flare into the sky." He pushed his right hand into the air, his index finger extending straight up. We boys started clapping and laughing.

Rosie stood up. "You're going to blow yourselves up for Fourth of July? You're Mexicans, not Americans. Hasn't this country done enough to you already?"

"Ask not what your country can do for you, but what you can do for your country," Dad said at the top of his lungs. "Right, boys?"

"Yeah!" we shouted.

Rosie shook her head and spun her finger in circles near her temple. "Estan locos," she muttered. My father and brothers and I all laughed.

Dad started walking out to Mom's rose garden, and we kids followed close behind.

"Boys, get away from your father," Mom shouted. "You could get hurt if that thing blows him up."

"Baby, it's just a grenade simulator," he said as he set it down at the edge of the rose garden.

"Hey, that thing isn't going to hurt my flowers, is it?" Mom asked.

"No, it's made out of paper. It's just like a big firecracker. All it does is go boom real loud. Kids, get on the porch with your mother. Now, all this thing does is make noise, but it can hurt your ears if you're too close, so stay on the porch and keep your ears covered. You all understand?" My brothers and I nodded, but Mom and Rosie just looked at each other and shook their heads.

Dad squatted down. "Okay, ready? One, two, three!" He pulled a pin, then ran to the porch and covered his ears. We watched carefully. The 200-watt army lightbulb on our front porch made the white grenade simulator look like a harmless ball of cotton. And then it went off with a massive *boom!* Rosie and Mom yelled and we all jumped back. Tiny pieces of white paper shot away from the explosion, and red rose petals floated to the ground in surrender. My brothers and I began jumping up and down in complete excitement. Our mother and Rosie ran to the garden and began gently picking up the fallen petals. Luckily for us only two roses blew up, but Mom was still mad.

"From now on, no more grenades!" she said. "Look what you've done to my roses!"

Dad held back his smile and threw his arms up. "Okay, honey, okay. I promise: No more grenades." Then he winked at us. Rosie held her hand to her chest as she picked up the fallen rose petals.

"Time for the flare," Dad announced. He walked to the

paper bag and took out the shiny pipe. All of us, including Mom and Rosie, followed Dad to the middle of the street. He slowly lifted off the top and positioned it on the bottom, gently pushing it into place. He made us kids stand a few feet behind him. Rosie began to cover her ears, but Mom told her that this one wasn't loud. Dad held the flare tightly in his left hand, fully extending his arm. He placed the palm of his right hand on the base of the flare.

He took some practice swings.

"Are you ready?" he asked us.

We jumped up. "Yes, yes!" we shouted.

"God bless America," he said. He slapped the base hard and *swoosh!* A white flash shot 200 feet up—a bright sword piercing the night sky. The flare lit up the whole neighborhood. It was brighter than all the army lightbulbs we could ever use. Its brilliance surrounded us, fading our brown skin.

Rosie shielded her eyes from the glare. "You all look like Americanos," she said.

She Flies

One of my earliest memories is of setting free more than 300 parakeets. It was my fifth birthday, and my parents had thrown me a party at Tía Mana Garza's house. Tía Mana had made me a dress and bought me matching shoes and a hat. She had decorated her backyard with ribbons tied to the trees and her two birdcages. One cage was filled with hundreds of parakeets. It was eight feet high and ten feet across, covered in chicken wire with holes so small that I could barely fit my little fingers through them. The other cage held Tía's favorite possession: a green and red parrot named Pájaro. Pájaro wore an ankle band attached to kite string so he wouldn't escape. Whenever Tía let him out of his cage, he walked to the top and stretched his wings. Sometimes he'd flutter them and then fly straight up at full speed, but the string would snap him down.

During my birthday party I walked up to the big parakeet cage with a cookie. I thought maybe I'd push the cookie under the cage door and see if the parakeets would eat it. Tía Mana had more colors in her big birdcage than there were in my biggest box of crayons. Some of the parakeets would fly back and forth really fast, hitting the cage with their bodies. Others would clutch the walls with their claws, and with their beaks they'd bite the cage wire. To me they looked as if they were trying to tear out of the cage. I think I felt sorry for them. Whenever I walked up to their cage, they turned their little heads and stared at me, fluttering their wings hard against the cage.

I turned around and looked at Tía Mana, who was watering her azaleas. She smiled at me but said nothing. I tried to push the cookie through the slit under the cage door, but it was too narrow. As I lifted the latch of the door, I heard my parents in the distance, telling me to stop. But I didn't want to stop.

I pulled the door open, and the sound of hundreds of singing birds swept away the shouts of my parents. The parakeets flew out, and I felt as if I were floating in a rainbow. They swirled around me, their feathers grazing my face, chest, shoulders, and arms. I wanted to float away with them. I could hear them whispering to me as they darted by. I lifted my arms and stood on the tips of my toes, wondering if I was about to fly. The birds swooped into the trees of Tía's backyard, singing happily. Pájaro, on his kite string, sang too. And Tía Mana dropped the water hose and put her arms up, as if she were trying to embrace the flying colors. She was laughing, and her laugh was the same pitch as that of the singing birds.

My father ran to me and slammed the cage door, but only a few birds still remained. He started yelling at me, but I couldn't understand him. He jabbed his finger inches from my face. I didn't know what he was so mad about. To me the parakeets wanted to be free, and Tía looked very happy watching them spread their tiny wings. I remember Dad saying that the birds were "escaping." It was the only word I heard, over and over.

Then I felt Tía Mana's hands on my stomach. I looked up and she was standing behind me. She pulled me to her, and I could feel her warmth on my back.

"Milagros has done the right thing," she said. "I've had those birds too long. They should be free."

For years afterward the parakeets lived in Tía Mana's backyard. Some flew to her neighbors' trees, but most made nests in her own. She had birds everywhere. Peacocks, ducks, and chickens walked freely in her yard, pecking here and there. She even had a turkey until it got run over by a car. My dad wanted to cook it, but Tía Mana wouldn't let him.

Her peacocks sometimes spread out their tails, showing off the rich hues of their plumes, but even *their* colors were not as bright as our dresses. When Tía Mana made a dress, she would buy enough flower-print fabric for both of us. We'd be covered in matching bright flowers, and long peacock feathers would hang from both our hats. Mom often joked that I was Tía's daughter, and we did look alike, especially when we dressed up. We both had dark brown eyes and smooth skin in the same brown tone, and Tía's hair was always as dark as mine.

Tía Mana lived across the street from us in a three-story house—the only three-story house in Weslaco. There were a few two-story homes across the railroad tracks, over on the west side, but Tía had the biggest house in Weslaco. Three of her cousins lived with her: Tía Bebe, Tía Ofelia, and Tía Conchita. Tía Mana was the oldest, and she worked as a midwife until she was eighty-five years old, the year I was born. I was the last baby she delivered, and she named me Milagros, because my mother was forty-five years old and wasn't supposed to have any more children. My mother told me that Tía Mana walked to St. Joan of Arc Catholic Church and lit a vela for me every day from the time she learned her niece was pregnant until I was born.

Tía Mana took care of me while my parents worked. I had an older brother and sister, but they were in high school and never had to baby-sit me. Every morning my mother carried me across the street to Tía's house, where I crawled to my delight, anywhere I wanted. My other tías worried that I'd fall down the stairs or get stuck under a bed. But Tía Mana told them that if her peacocks, ducks, and chickens could walk anywhere they wanted, so could I, and that if I had wings, she'd let me fly.

The second floor of Tía's house was surrounded by a

balcony, and every afternoon when I walked home from first grade, there she'd be in one of her colorful dresses, waving to me from the balcony. I'd walk up to see her, and we'd share a glass of iced red, purple, or green Kool-Aid. I liked all the colors, but my favorite was green, with fresh pineapple slices floating in it. We'd sit in her blue metal chairs, gently rocking to the rhythm of swaying palm trees, and we'd search for faces in the clouds floating in from Mexico. Pájaro would search with us.

Pájaro had been Tía's parrot since she was a young woman. She said he had lived so long because he received Holy Communion every week. On Sundays when Tía went to church, she always got an extra host from the priest for Pájaro. The bird loved to eat the host and never forgot to thank God for it. "Gracias a Diosito," he'd say.

Pájaro was very smart. He'd take food from my hand without snapping and say, "Gracias, muy bueno." I'd pet his forehead and stroke his feathers and he'd say, "*Rrrrrrrrrrr, ooooo* sí" as he fluttered his wings. Tía let Pájaro walk around the balcony, since he had the string tied to his ankle bracelet. It was a long string, and Pájaro would walk back and forth from one end of the railing to the other, complimenting himself with, "Qué güapo soy yo." Tía would smile and nod at each phrase the bird spoke.

"That's what your grandfather used to say when he got all dressed up for a dance," she'd tell me. "And he was right: He *was* a handsome man, my brother."

Pájaro held the voices of Tía's memories and of our family. I told Tía I wanted her to teach Pájaro how to say, "Kool-Aid is good," and she said that she'd do her best, but that Pájaro was a Mexican bird and liked to speak Spanish.

It was a family tradition to have birthday parties at Tía's house, but Tía went out of her way to make my parties bigger than all the others. My tenth birthday was no exception, and we celebrated my parents' thirty-fifth wedding anniversary that day too. Tía made me a bright dress and a cake with the same colors. She invited everyone from the neighborhood, all my cousins, and lots of my school friends. My dad and tíos cooked fajitas, and a couple of uncles brought their guitars and accordions.

After dinner my uncles played "Happy Birthday" on their accordions, and everyone sang as I stood in front of my cake. The cake had ten candles on it, plus little plastic statues of a bride and groom for my parents. Tía Mana leaned toward me and asked, "What are you going to wish for?"

"I don't know," I said. "What do you think I should wish for?"

I felt her warm breath in my ear. "A plane ticket to anywhere you want to go."

I must have looked surprised but hopeful. Tía put her hand on my shoulder. "Don't tell anybody yet, but I got you two gift certificates so you and your mother can go anywhere you want in the country."

The music stopped, and I heard people telling me to

make a wish. I looked at my tía and said out loud, "I wish I could fly somewhere." I took in a big breath and blew out all ten candles while the plastic bride and groom watched me.

My tías had pitched in and bought me a piñata in the shape of King Kong, and it took my big brother to bash it open. Candy and peanuts scattered everywhere. All my friends and cousins dove to the ground, scrambling to collect as much candy as they could stuff into their pockets. The peacocks, ducks, and chickens scrambled for the peanuts.

By ten o'clock my tíos had everybody dancing. Tía asked two of my older primos to carry Pájaro's cage from the front balcony to the back so the bird could watch the party. She tied the string around Pájaro's ankle and let him come out of the cage. He flew to the railing and looked down on the dancers. My relatives smiled and called out to him, and he made repetitive squawking sounds, as if he were laughing. He spread his wings and shouted down to the dancers, "Bailamos, viejos!"

Tía laughed and held her hands together. "Ah, tu tía Carmen. She loved to make fun of the old men." She smiled at me and took my hand. "Let's go join them."

I danced all night with my primos, primas, tíos, tías, my father, and even my brother and sister. My parents said that I fell asleep on the balcony in one of the metal chairs and that Pájaro sat on the armrest, singing, "Ru, ru, ru, ru."

The following day Tía Mana showed my mother and me the airline gift certificates she'd bought us. They were for 300 dollars each, and we could use them anytime we wanted.

My mother held the certificates and shook her head. "I don't think your father will let us fly anywhere," she said to me.

"Why not? This is a present from Tía," I said.

"Well, where do you want to fly?" she asked.

"Somewhere far. Like California!" I said, excited at the thought.

"No, Milagros, you're too young to go so far away," Mom answered. "How about flying to San Antonio or Houston to visit your cousins there?"

Tía Mana frowned. "You could *drive* to San Antonio or Houston," she said. "I bought these tickets so you could take Milagros somewhere far away. Somewhere new. Just the two of you."

"No, I don't think her father would let us go somewhere far," my mother said again.

"I don't want to go to San Antonio or Houston," I insisted. "I want to go somewhere far away."

Mom sighed and looked over the gift certificates. "I'll tell you what," she said. "These don't look like they have an expiration date. I'll keep them safe, and when you're a little older, maybe you can go somewhere on your own."

I didn't like that deal but there was nothing I could do. "Okay, but I want Tía Mana to keep the tickets," I said.

Tía nodded. "Bueno, then I will hold them." She turned to my mother. "When Milagros turns into a young woman, she will make her own decisions."

For my quinceañera Tía made me a white satin dress

with lace around the edges. It was as beautiful as a wedding dress. Pájaro thought so too. When I modeled it for him, his eyes got big, and he started turning in circles on the railing, saying, "No te cases! No te cases!"

Tía shook her head. "Pájaro, it's her quinceañera, not her wedding day." She shook her finger at him. "You never forget anything, do you, old bird?"

Tía explained that many years before, lots of handsome men wanted to marry her. She said they'd come over to the house, sit on the balcony, and watch the sunset with her. "Back then there was just the church and fields all around the house," she said. "My father owned more than two hundred acres of land, and everyone wanted to buy, but he wouldn't sell." Then her father was killed in a hunting accident. "Shot right through the head," she said. The land became hers and her two brothers'. But her brothers were killed in World War I, so the land became hers, and all kinds of men suddenly wanted to meet her. Some wanted to marry her; others wanted to take her hunting.

"You watch those men," she told me. "Some of them try to keep you from things. Don't you let them!"

My mother never went anywhere without her husband, but I liked to go places without asking, and that's why Dad had my window screen nailed down the night of my quinceañera party. After the party I had gone home and changed into jeans and a T-shirt, then sneaked out of the house. My friends and I drove around awhile, but we didn't drink or do anything wild. When I got home, way after midnight, I found the window screen nailed shut and my father staring angrily through it. He shouted for me to go to the front door.

Dad opened the door, scowling. Mom was sitting behind him on the living room couch. "Your mother told me that Tía Mana bought you some plane tickets a few years ago," Dad said. "I was going to let you go on a trip for your birthday this year; it was going to be a surprise. But after this, you can just forget about flying anywhere."

I looked at my mother, hoping she would jump in and say something, but she didn't, and I knew there was no sense in fighting about it.

"You have anything to say?" Dad asked.

I gave him the right answer. "I'm sorry I sneaked out of the house. I won't do it again."

"Then go to bed. We're glad you're okay. You had us worried," he said. Before I fell asleep, I thanked God that Tía had the plane tickets, because my mother would have given them to Dad.

A couple of months after my quinceañera Tía Mana turned 100 years old. She was excited because she'd be able to have her picture shown on the *Today* show. She said she never saw Mexican Americans on American TV unless they were being arrested for something. She wanted me to take a picture of her and send it in. I brought home a digital camera I used for the yearbook and took several pictures of Tía Mana smiling, with Pájaro on her shoulder. I downloaded the images and showed her and Pájaro the hard copies I'd printed out. Pájaro squawked and hung upside down in his cage, which Tía said was a good sign. She picked the photo she liked and I e-mailed it to the *Today* show, along with Tía's birthday, her full name—Juanita Salinas-Garza—her address, and Pájaro's name.

On Tía's birthday my whole family sat around the TV, waiting and hoping for the announcement. My father set the VCR to record the show. When the segment with the weatherman came on, Tía put her hands together in hope. Then there, filling the screen, were Tía's and Pájaro's faces! The weatherman mispronounced every name—Tía's, Pájaro's, and even our town, Weslaco. We played that tape many times and laughed and laughed. Even Pájaro thought it was funny. He kept saying, "Hombre loco" over and over.

"Milagros," Tía Mana said, "I'm going to send you to New York City so you can tell that man how to say our names right."

The thought of going to New York City had never entered my mind, but Tía's joke made it sound so immediate, so easy—as if the plane were ready to take off and all I had to do was say, "When?"

So I did. "When?" I asked with excitement.

Tía laughed. "Whenever you're ready," she answered, holding her arms out.

My dad stood up from his chair. "She's not going to New York City," he said. "She's staying here."

Tía Mana raised her brow. "She can go if she wants to,"

she said. "She needs to teach that man on TV how to say things right." My other tías started laughing. Even my mother laughed, though she kept her hand over her mouth. My father sat back down, seething.

I brought Julian, a boy I liked, to Tía Mana's 100th birthday party. All Julian wanted to do was make out on the balcony where people couldn't see us, and after an hour of trying to keep his grabbing hands off me, I began to think he was gross.

Tía didn't like him much either. At one point she called us over to her so that Julian could take a better look at Pájaro, who was out of his cage. "Doesn't Pájaro have pretty eyes?" she said to him.

Julian leaned toward Pájaro and said in a baby voice, "Polly wanna cracker?" Pájaro answered with a loud squawk. Julian chuckled, turned slightly to me, and said in a condescending tone, "This bird thinks he can talk."

Just then Pájaro spread his wings, lunged, and bit Julian right on the nose. "Feo," the bird yelled. Julian pulled back, covering his nose, and Pajaro flapped his wings, shouting, "Feo, feo" as he turned in circles. I could tell that Tía wanted to laugh, but she pressed her lips tight and looked at the ground. Not me; I threw my head back and laughed with abandon. I realized that Pájaro was a better judge of character than I was.

We sent Julian home with a piece of cake and a bag of ice, and I danced the rest of the night with my family.

That year Tía started telling me that she would help me if I went to college. She had made the same offer to my brother, sister, and cousins, but no one had yet taken her up on it. My brother joined the army, and my sister got pregnant her senior year and married her boyfriend.

All through high school I managed to stay in honors classes, so Tía urged me to apply to a good college. She knew I needed encouragement to follow my dreams, so whenever I mentioned a state school, she would frown and say, "It's a big country. You should go somewhere different for a while." She would take the atlas off her bookshelf and open it to the map of the United States, and we would measure the distance between Weslaco and other cities across the country. Tía always pointed to the farthest corners. "Mi'ja, fly as far as your wings will take you. You can always come back," she'd say.

I took my SATs and scored a 1260, and schools I'd never heard of, from far-off parts of the country, started sending brochures and applications to my house. My parents tried to convince me that there were plenty of schools in Texas that were just as good and less expensive. When I explained that the out-of-state schools were offering scholarships and grants, my parents warned that the grants would cover only some of the cost. I told them that Tía had offered to pay some of my college expenses, but they said she needed that money for the nursing home. It was the first I'd heard of a nursing home.

"You can't put Tía in a nursing home," I cried.

"Well, who's going to take care of her?" my father said. "If you're far away at school, you can't do it, and we both have our jobs."

"But there's nothing wrong with her," I said. "She has never been sick, and she does everything by herself."

"Sí, pero she's a hundred and two," my mother said. "She's already been on that *Today* show three times. You think she's going to live forever?"

Dad added, "She can't drive anymore and her eyesight is going bad. And you're the only one who spends time with her."

"But she has the tías. They can take care of her. They're younger."

"Milagros, they're in their eighties. They can't even take care of themselves," Dad argued. "So if you're going to leave the Valley, don't be surprised to come home and find all your tías in a nursing home." My eyes began watering and my father backed off, but I could tell he was pleased to have made his point.

That night I lay in bed, worrying about Tía. What if she fell down the stairs and I was far away at some college? I knew my family would take care of her, but I was the one she trusted. And what would happen to Pájaro? I tossed and turned. There was a university twenty miles away that I could attend and still take care of Tía, but I had my heart set on going somewhere new and unfamiliar. I looked out my bedroom window at my tía's house, and I wondered if she and Pájaro were able to sleep.

At school the next day I looked over the glossy brochure for a college in Vermont. I imagined my tías in a nursing home and Pájaro in a cage with no one to talk to, all because I wanted to go to some distant college where it snowed in the winter. I thought maybe I could take Pájaro with me, but then he might catch pneumonia and die. I hadn't even been accepted to any of the colleges yet, but I couldn't seem to stop worrying.

That afternoon I sat outside on the balcony with my tía, drinking Kool-Aid and letting the setting Valley sun bathe me. I watched Tía, looking for any signs that she was slowing down.

"How are you feeling today, Tía Mana?" I asked, trying not to sound too concerned.

"Every day is another day," she said. She put down her glass of Kool-Aid and looked at me. "Mi'jita, I have known you all your life, and I know when you are troubled. Bueno, dime. What's wrong?"

I walked to the railing and let out a sigh. "Ay, Tía. It's just that Mom and Dad said I shouldn't go far away to college. They think I should stay here and take care of you."

Tía chuckled. "Take care of me? I can take care of myself."

"Sí, Tía, but they say you are getting old, y que . . ." I tried to find the words.

"Estoy vieja." She laughed. "Mira, I can take care of myself. I always have. They don't want you to go away because *they* never went anywhere."

"But if you *do* get to a point where you can't take care of yourself, they'll put you in a nursing home," I told her. "Y Tía, I would feel terrible if that happened. I don't want you in a nursing home, and what would happen to Pájaro?"

I heard a car, and looked over the railing to where my parents were pulling into our driveway. My father had a loud diesel truck, and Tía knew the noise it made. "Is that your father's truck?" she asked.

"Yeah, they just drove up."

"Call them over here," Tía said in a firm voice. "I need to talk to them."

I looked at Tía, but she just turned and shouted through the screen door for the other tías to come out. When she wanted to discuss something, Tía Mana liked to have the other tías around. They talked about everything as if they were a committee.

I waved down at my parents and they waved back, and then I yelled out that Tía Mana wanted to see them. I could tell they weren't happy about it, but they never ignored Tía's requests.

By the time my parents got up to the balcony, the other tías were outside waiting patiently, their metal chairs positioned in a semicircle. Mom and Dad smiled and hugged all the tías. Dad went inside the house and brought out two chairs for himself and Mom, and they joined the committee. They had sat in on enough of Tía's meetings to know the routine: Shut up and listen. Tía Mana offered my parents Kool-Aid and they each took a glass, though they never drank Kool-Aid.

Then Tía began. "Doesn't Pájaro have pretty feathers?" she said.

"Oh, yes, beautiful feathers," my mom said.

"Y sabes qué? Pájaro can fly. Pero I always tie a string around his ankle because I'm afraid if I let him go, he'll fly away and never come back. Sí, sí." Tía rocked in her chair gently. "I'm afraid of losing him. But if you have beautiful wings, you were meant to fly, no?"

Tía Mana waited for an answer. My mother and father looked at each other, their faces a mix of annoyance and anxiety. They nodded at Tía, and my other tías nodded as well.

"Diosito gives everyone gifts, and it's a sin not to use them," Tía Olivia said with conviction.

"Y también, it's a sin not to let people use the gifts Diosito blessed them with," Tía Mana said. All the tías nodded again, saying, "Sí, sí, es la verdad." Tía Mana looked at my parents. "No?"

My parents nodded. "Sí, Tía, it's a sin," my mother agreed.

It was quiet for a moment and Pájaro fluttered his wings.

"I love Pájaro more than most anything else," Tía Mana said. "This bird has brought so much happiness. I've had him for more than seventy years, and he knows all about our family." She pointed to my parents. "He watched you two get married and has seen the birth of all three of your children. Sí, I love this bird, pero I have kept him in a cage all this time. Eso no es amor. No, love does not cage. Love sets free."

All my tías nodded, and Tía Olivia patted her heart and said, "You cannot hold love."

"I love only one person more than I love this bird. I love Milagros, pero I want her to be happy. To be free." Tía Mana wiped a tear from her cheek.

She looked at me, smiled, and gestured for me to walk over to Pájaro's cage.

"Mi'ja, open Pájaro's cage," she whispered.

I hesitated. The string wasn't attached to his ankle bracelet.

"Go ahead, mi'ja, open it," Tía urged me.

I opened the cage door wide, and Pájaro blinked at me, confused. I reached in, took off his ankle bracelet, and stepped back. Pájaro jumped from his mesquite branch to the edge of the birdcage door and started to flutter his wings. My parents stood up. I could hear them saying, "Close the door," but they sounded far away. My tías looked blissful. Pájaro squawked, and he climbed to the top of the cage. Then he pushed off, saying, "Milagros, qué bonita," and started to sing. He flew toward me, and I could feel the brush of feathers—hundreds and hundreds of feathers as parakeets of every color kissed me good-bye. Hundreds of parakeets, singing, and Tía Mana on the tips of her toes, throwing her arms up. Calling to us, "Fly, fly, fly."

The California Cousins

The first thing our California cousins said when they stepped out of their car was that their butts were asleep. It wasn't an auspicious start to the visit. It had been three years since we'd seen Tía Alice, Tío Mike, and our cousins. The last time I was only seven, but I remember that Tío Mike got into a fight with Dad, and it took all our bigger cousins and tíos to get them apart. I'm not sure who started the fight, but from that moment on, my brother and I didn't care for our California cousins. But Tía Alice was Mom's little sister and they were very close, so we couldn't avoid the occasional visit.

When Mom told us they were coming to stay with us, even Dad was unhappy. "Honey, that's the week we're taking the kids to Astroworld," he said.

"Yeah, Mom," I said. "You promised two whole days at Astroworld."

"Can't they come two weeks later?" Juan asked.

Mom knew we were disappointed and could also see that Dad was looking for a way out. "Okay, let's make a deal. What if your father and I buy you guys a brand-new minibike?"

We all shouted "Minibike!"—Juan and I with excitement, and Dad with a what-about-me? tone.

"You can buy a new fishing rod and go fishing with your friends for a whole weekend," Mom said to Dad. "But hey! All of you better be extra nice to our California cousins, and that means you too, honey."

Mom said it took three days to drive from Bakersfield to the Valley, so that was how much time we had to clean up the whole house, inside and out, or no minibike and no fishing rod.

"Why?" Juan and I said. "We never clean the house when our cousins from San Antonio or Houston come to visit us."

"That's right," Dad said. Mom shot him a look, and he quickly backed down like our dog when we yelled at him.

"That's different. They live in Texas; they're used to seeing houses like ours," Mom said. "In California they have nice houses."

We lived on Mile 13½ on an acre of land, surrounded by cabbage fields. Ours was a dirt road, so every time a car drove past, dust covered the front of our house. Mom actually made us hose down the house to get the dust off. We washed the windows and cut the grass, and we helped Mom plant flowers all around the house and trees. We repainted all the trees a bright white, fixed our broken swing, and put up a hammock that we'd bought in Las Flores, México.

Dad and his friend tried to start our other car, which had been parked at the side of the house for months. Dad always liked us to watch him when he was working on our cars. He promised me that when I turned eleven, he would teach me how to drive, but first I had to learn how to *fix* cars. Juan was nine but Dad promised him too: If he learned about cars, then he too would get driving lessons when I turned eleven. We'd stand with devotion next to Dad as he worked, fighting over which of us got to pass him the tools he needed: screwdrivers, wrenches, pliers, hammers, duct tape, and coat hangers. The day before our cousins arrived, we watched Dad and his friend work on the car for what seemed like hours. They couldn't get it started, so they finally tied a rope to it and pulled it to someone else's house.

Mom even had us fix up the outhouse. We put in new nails where some were missing, and with the paint left over from the trees, we painted the outside walls. She had bought some sandpaper and made us sand down the toilet seat, and to us, that was the craziest chore of all. We had cut the grass, planted, scrubbed, waxed, fixed, painted, wiped, swept, washed dishes, washed clothes, washed our dog (couldn't catch the cat), and gotten haircuts. And now we were sanding down the toilet seat.

"Why are we doing this?" I asked her.

"I don't want them getting splinters in their butts," Mom

said as she shook a can of Glade springtime-scent air freshener.

"We never get splinters in *our* butts," Juan said.

"That's because you have rough butts," she answered, spraying more of the Glade in the little room, making us cough and sneeze. "And while your cousins are here, don't use the bathroom inside the house. You two can use only this one."

"But—" Juan started.

"No buts," Mom said, and she walked off.

We looked at each other and made California butt jokes under our breath as we sweated over the smooth wood.

"What a bunch of sissy soft-butts," Juan said.

"Hey, it's worth a brand-new minibike," I told him.

Our California cousins were older and bigger than us, and when we walked up to greet them, they didn't hug us. Jordan had been driving the car, with his father in the passenger seat. He was going into his senior year in high school, and was six feet tall. His hair was slicked back, he had a small goatee right under his lip, and he was wearing wraparound mirrored sunglasses. His brother, Todd, was going into his junior year and was just as tall, with a thin moustache and a white straw hat. Tiffany, their sister, was going into her freshman year. She was wearing Ray-Ban sunglasses and had platinum blonde hair and long fingernails painted gold. None of them seemed too happy to see us, but we had lots planned for them; we were determined to have fun.

Tía Alice gave Juan and me big hugs and handed us each a bag of nuts from the factory where she worked. She and Mom hugged each other and talked a mile a minute while Tío Mike stood by silently, looking mean and fussing with the collar of his black guayabera. He wore dark sunglasses and had a full goatee, and there was a tattoo on his forearm of a cross with weird letters on it. He didn't hug us, but when Tía Alice urged him, he shook our hands and gave Mom a hug. After a pause he shook Dad's hand too, but he didn't smile. Dad was just as cool back.

We all went inside the house where we had a window air conditioner, and we had a lunch of fideo, rice, and beans. There wasn't much conversation among us, so Tía Alice and Mom talked and answered for all of us. After we ate, Mom gave Juan and me the signal to entertain our cousins. We asked them if they wanted to go outside, but Tiffany said it was too hot and she'd rather sit in the air-conditioned room. We looked at Jordan and Todd. They didn't say anything.

"Why don't you go outside and play with your cousins?" Tía Alice said to them.

Todd grimaced and adjusted his straw hat. "It's hot outside. It's like Death Valley or something," he said.

"Well, it's about time you put that hat to good use," his mother answered with a gentle laugh. "Now, go outside and play with your cousins." Todd and Jordan both sighed, then stood up slowly and followed us.

We walked outside, and Todd pointed to the trees and

asked why they were white. We told him that the paint keeps the gusanos off.

"The what?" Jordan said.

We told them again, but they didn't know what the word *gusano* meant. They said they didn't speak Spanish.

"The *worms*," I said. "The paint keeps the worms off."

Jordan and Todd started laughing. "That's stupid," Todd said. "How is this white paint going to keep worms off the trees?"

Juan and I shrugged, because we had no idea how it worked. Juan pointed up to the branches. "You don't see any worms up there, do you? See, it works."

Jordan began walking toward the outhouse.

"What's this? Your little clubhouse?" he said sneeringly. He opened the door and looked inside, then covered his nose and said to his brother, "Dude, they use this thing to go to the bathroom." Both cousins started laughing.

"Yeah, we all do," I said.

"Even Uncle Roy and Aunt Mary?" Todd asked.

"Yeah," my brother answered. "If the bathroom inside the house is being used, you can always use this one."

Jordan and Todd kept looking inside the outhouse and laughing. My brother didn't look happy.

"You guys live like the Beverly Hillbillies," Jordan said.

My brother and I looked at each other and shook our heads because we didn't know who the Beverly Hillbillies were.

"Hey," my brother said, "we even sanded down the toilet

seat so you wouldn't get splinters in your soft California butts."

Jordan looked down at Juan. "Hey, little dude, you better watch what you say. We're bigger than you, because all you little Mexicans eat down here is rice and beans. In California we eat *real* food. Even when you dudes get to high school, you'll still be little *Texas* Mexicans."

We clenched our fists, and Todd stepped in. "Okay, okay, cool it, man, they're just little kids," he said. "All right, dudes, what else do you have around here?"

We knew we had to be calm, because getting into a fight with them would surely cost us the minibike. We took them out to the canal to throw rocks at cans and bottles. We hoped we'd find some sapos (we had to translate *sapo* to *toad* for them) or a turtle or even catch a fish.

"Hey, dudes, there is no way you're going to find anything alive in that green Texas water," Todd said.

"You dudes are probably short because you drink this green stuff," Jordan said.

Next we took them to the monte to walk around, but Todd brushed up against some cactus and whined about the little espinas in his leg.

Then we took them to the railroad tracks by the abandoned grain elevators, where we could climb on the rusted railcars. "Hey, dudes, those train cars are covered in rust," Jordan said. "I'm not going to get my threads dirty."

So we took them to the burned-down ice factory to look for treasure. But they thought that was dumb too. Nothing we showed them made them happy, and they weren't thrilling us either.

Walking back home on the dirt road, they kept complaining.

"So, you little dudes live out here in the middle of nowhere. No malls, no freeways, no buildings, no nothing," Todd said.

"Where we're from we got everything," Jordan said. "Freeways, airports, stadiums to watch football, basketball, and baseball. We got big malls and big movie theaters and big mountains. We got everything."

"You little dudes don't even have real bathrooms," Todd said. "You have to go outside like a bunch of dogs." He started laughing, and Jordan started making fart sounds.

My brother snapped. "At least we're not a bunch of California soft-butt crybabies like you and your whole family!" Juan started mimicking them in a high-pitched girl's voice. "It's too hot! I might get my clothes dirty. Ouch, the espinas hurt my leg!"

I told Juan to cálmate, but it was too late. Todd pushed him to the ground, and I tried to take on Jordan. I pushed him, but he didn't budge. He laughed and shoved me into the dirt.

"You little dudes better not try that again," Jordan said, but we were up again and down just as fast.

"You guys are like Uncle Roy," Todd said. "Stubborn and small." Juan tried to get up, but I pulled him back. Jordan and Todd walked off, laughing and making fart sounds.

We waited until they were long gone, then stood up and dusted ourselves off.

"Do you still want the minibike?" Juan asked.

"I'd rather walk," I said.

We spent an hour throwing rocks into the canal, trying to think of how to get back at our California cousins. We thought of throwing rocks at *them,* putting ants in their beds or tacks on the floor of the bedroom, sneaking Ex-Lax into their food, and cutting the ropes on our swing and hammock so they'd fall. But we figured we'd get caught too easily. Then we thought of our neighbors' dog, Cuete. Cuete got his name because he could eat firecrackers that were lit, and if the cuete went off in his mouth, he didn't even cry. Cuete was a mean dog and wasn't afraid of anything. He'd bitten me twice in the leg and my brother once in the butt. We thought of luring the cousins to the neighbors' house so Cuete would bite their butts off, but then Cuete might bite us too. That dog didn't care *who* he bit.

We thought of shooting bottle rockets at our cousins. We had a plastic pipe we used to launch our bottle rockets at dogs, cats, and each other, but it wasn't accurate enough. Juan suggested we wait until one of them used the outhouse and then throw a bunch of bottle rockets in there. We thought that would be funny—bottle rockets flying all over the place. The guy wouldn't stand a chance. Ah, but if he lost an eye . . . n'hombre, no. We'd never hear the end of it.

Then we figured out the perfect plan. We would take three cuetes and tape them under the outhouse's toilet seat.

Right where the side of the butt meets the edge of the seat. We'd make a long fuse and wait until one of the cousins used the toilet. Juan wanted to tape a bottle rocket instead of a cuete so all the shooting sparks would burn their butts off, but we decided that blowing up their butts would be funnier.

We didn't sleep in the house that night. We told our parents we were going to camp outside in our tent so our cousins could sleep in our beds. Juan went into our room and took out the shoe box we'd filled with ten packs of 100 cuetes each. We stayed up for hours that night, unraveling cuetes and tying all the short fuses together. One of us would unravel while the other held the flashlight. It was painstaking professional work, but we had learned to make square knots in the Cub Scouts, so we knew what we were doing.

By three in the morning we had unraveled all but three of the cuetes and had a six-foot fuse. We found a crack at the back of the outhouse, threaded the fuse through it, and connected it to the short fuses of the three remaining cuetes. We taped the cuetes underneath the seat with a thin strip of duct tape and threw all the remaining evidence into the toilet.

Dad woke us up at eight in the morning and asked if we wanted breakfast, but we said we weren't hungry. We spent the whole day outside while the cousins stayed in the air-conditioned room watching TV. We tossed a football back and forth and lay in the hammock, waiting for one of them to come out to use the bathroom.

At one o'clock Todd came out and went into the outhouse. Juan ran to the fuse with his matches, and I ran to see whether Todd's toes were facing the toilet or me. His toes faced the toilet, and I could hear him peeing. I worried that he couldn't aim right. When Todd was finished, Juan and I checked the fuse and the cuetes, and we were happy to find that our hard work was still dry.

At eight, as the sun was setting, Jordan came out. He looked at us and made a fart sound. We didn't say anything. Once the door to the outhouse was closed, we got into our positions. Jordan's toes faced me. I looked at Juan and grinned. The fuse sparkled brilliantly as it disappeared into the darkness of the outhouse. We ran to the hammock and waited, and then palo! We jumped with glee, and Jordan came running out screaming, his pants and underwear down to his knees.

Juan and I pointed at him and laughed louder than all the cuetes going off. Everyone came out of the house, and Mom and Tía Alice ran over to Jordan. We could see a bright red spot on the side of his butt.

"Qué hicieron?" our mother demanded.

"Qué? We didn't do nothing," we said with our arms up, showing our empty hands. Mom and Dad ordered us inside, into their bedroom. After a few threats involving a belt, we came clean.

Dad laughed, but Mom was fast. "It's not funny," she said. Dad covered his mouth and shook his head, but we could see he wanted to keep laughing.

"Mom, it was just a cuete. He's just being a big baby," Juan said.

"Estan locos? You could have blown up the outhouse!" Mom yelled.

"It was just a cuete, Mom," I said. "How can one cuete blow up the outhouse?"

"Because there's methane gas in there," she said.

My brother and I looked puzzled. "What?" I asked.

"Methane gas. It's highly explosive. It comes from caca," she said. "You could have blown up the whole outhouse." Dad raised his brow and nodded.

"Methane gas," Juan said.

"Yes, methane gas. It's very explosive. It comes from caca," Mom repeated.

The meaning of her words slowly dawned on us. My brother and I turned to each other and tried to hold back our grins. We could see the outhouse exploding into a million pieces. Throwing caca everywhere. Our chests contracted, and the air flowed through our vocal cords, gently pushing the glorious words out of our mouths, and we said in awed brotherly harmony, *"Methane gas."*

Dad burst out laughing.

Last Mass

I am the third-best, third-most reluctant altar boy Santa Theresa church has ever known. I was eight years old when Father Bob announced at Sunday mass that the church needed altar boys. I slid down in my seat so the priest wouldn't see me, but my father stood up. He was the mayor of Edcouch and it was an election year, so he said, "Father Bob, my son Pedro would like to sign up to be an altar boy," and he patted my shoulder with pride.

My mother smiled and my ten-year-old sister smirked. "You're going to wear a dress," she said through her hand that could barely hide her delight.

The priest smiled. "Good, Mr. Reyes, thank you. And if any other boys are interested, please see me after mass."

Four other boys volunteered: Roel, who was the son of the police chief, Homer and Julio, the sons of the city manager, and Miguel, the son of the woman who cleaned the church. I was the youngest by three years, and the smallest.

We stood outside the church while Father Bob shook hands with the departing parishioners. My father, the police chief, and the city manager were also shaking hands with the people leaving the church. They talked louder than anyone else and laughed twice as loudly. Miguel and his mother sat on a bench and spoke softly to each other.

Father Bob invited us back into the church and made us sit in a row in the first pew. He introduced his two current altar boys, who were seniors in high school and were graduating. They were both a foot taller than the priest, and each had a moustache, and they stood on either side of him with their arms crossed, as if they were his bodyguards. They had thick necks and wide shoulders, and they wore black T-shirts, blue jeans, and black cowboy boots. They scowled at us, their hands in fists as if they were ready to fight. My mother had once told me that they had been caught stealing and that the judge had given them the choice of serving as altar boys for three years or going to juvenile detention for that time.

"These are my altar boys," Father Bob said. "Ricardo Sangre and José Mata." They didn't move. "Maybe you've seen them play football? They're offensive players. They're very good," he said with a smile. But then a trace of disappointment flashed across his face. "Well, Ricardo used to play, but he has been suspended for fighting. He sent a get-well card, though, and he has asked God for forgiveness, and God forgives anyone who asks." Ricardo let out a deep breath and his forearm muscles flexed. Father Bob went on to explain that Ricardo and José knew everything about the church and that they would train us over the next few weeks.

Roel snapped his chewing gum, and it echoed in the empty church. Ricardo's right arm swung out fast, and he pointed at Roel. "Hey, this is the house of our Lord Jesus Christ, not *your* house," he said, continuing to point. "No chewing gum in church. Ever."

Father Bob patted Ricardo on the shoulder. "Thank you, Ricky," he said. Ricardo returned to his bodyguard position.

"Any questions?" Father Bob asked with a smile as his gaze swept across us. None of us said anything. He clapped his hands. "Very well, then." Turning to Ricardo and José, he asked, "Is Tuesday good for you two?" They didn't respond. "Then it's settled. We'll see you boys at five o'clock on Tuesday for altar boy training."

Two days later we had our first altar boy meeting, but only Miguel and I showed up. The other three said they had baseball practice and promised to come to the next meeting, but they never came to any. I got to church before Miguel did and sat outside on the bench, waiting for Ricardo and José. When Miguel walked up, he asked why I was waiting outside.

"Is the church open?" I asked.

"The church is always open," he said. "Let's go inside and wait in the air-conditioning."

We walked in, and I stopped at the entrance for a moment. There was no one there. It was soothingly dim, cool, and very quiet. I could smell the scent of all the lit velas—dozens of them, their flames making the glossy skin of the Mary and Jesus statues glow. And the afternoon sun was taking its late stroll through the stained-glass windows, reflecting the blues, greens, and reds onto the marble floor.

Miguel saw a tissue and some church bulletins on the floor, and he started to pick them up. "These people just leave things all over the floor," he said.

I sat down in the pew my family always sat in, and I leaned back and hoped that Ricardo and José had forgotten our meeting. Miguel walked around the church, picking up bulletins and candy wrappers. I studied one of the stations of the cross that surrounded the inside of the church. The station I was looking at showed Christ carrying the cross, and I noticed the fine detail on the plaster cast: Christ had a bony back, but he must have been pretty strong.

Miguel called out to me from the front of the altar. "Hey, come on. Let's go see if the guys are in the little room back here." He pointed behind the wall that had the large crucifix hanging on it. Father Bob would often disappear behind that wall after mass.

"Won't we get in trouble if we go back there?" I asked.

"N'hombre, my mother and I go back there all the time to clean it. It's just a room with the priest's clothes and stuff."

I followed him around the wall. It was dark, and the door was closed. Miguel put his ear to the door.

"Do you hear anything?" I whispered.

Miguel shook his head, then turned the knob and slowly opened the door. He flipped a switch on the wall, and white fluorescent lights came on.

The center of the room had a table with a big Bible on it. There were crosses on the wall and two 3-D images of Christ. One image showed Christ smiling when you looked at him head-on, but when you walked to the side and looked again, he was crying and had a crown of thorns around his head. In the corner were a kitchen sink, a refrigerator with bottles of wine on top of it, and a microwave oven. An unopened box of popcorn bags sat next to the microwave. One wall held a closet; one of the doors was open, and lots of black robes were hanging inside.

We could hear talking through a back door, and we approached it carefully. I put my ear to the door.

"Open it," Miguel said. "See who it is."

"I think it's them. *You* open it," I said.

"They don't like me. Every time I come with my mother to clean, they make fun of me."

"Well, I'm not going to open it. I don't even want to be an altar boy."

Suddenly the talking stopped outside the door. Miguel and I looked at each other, and he pointed to the front door and mouthed, "Let's go." But it was too late. The back door swung open, and there were Ricardo and José, smoking cigarettes.

Our first thought was to run, and we jerked around as if

we were going to, but José shouted, "Stop! If you two run, we'll catch you and beat the crap out of you."

We froze in fear. Ricardo and José stood outside the doorway, blocking the afternoon sun. They both took a final drag, blew the smoke out of their noses, and threw their cigarettes behind them. Ricardo walked through the door first, stopped, and crossed his arms. José stood next to him in the same position.

"What are you doing here?" Ricardo asked. Miguel and I looked at each other nervously and said nothing.

"Hey, he asked you a question," José said. Both of their expressions seemed to say that if we gave them the wrong answer, they'd beat us up and throw us in the canal that ran behind the church.

"F-F-Father Bob said to come here. That you'd train us to be altar boys," I stuttered.

José nodded and put his hands on his hips. "Ah, sí, you two want to be altar boys." He tapped Ricardo on the shoulder. "The son of the cleaning woman and the son del mayor want to be altar boys."

"Pues bueno, let's get started," Ricardo said to us.

"Does the priest let you guys smoke in this room?" Miguel asked.

"Hey! First rule: Shut up," José said as he pointed to us. I jumped at his shout. Miguel and I took a half step toward each other. "You got it? Shut up. You just listen. If you have any questions, they better not be stupid ones or we'll beat the hell out of you."

Ricardo then stepped forward. "Second rule: Everything in the church has a name. This is not a *room*. It's the sacristy, and no, we don't smoke in the sacristy. We don't smoke anywhere in the church."

José nodded. "Orale, let's get going. Mass starts at six, and the church has to be ready."

They gave us a tour of the sacristy and told us not to touch anything unless we asked first, and that if we did ask, the answer would be no. Ricardo showed us the closet with the priest's and altar boys' clothes all hanging in two neat rows.

"These are called vestments," Ricardo said. He took out a black robe and a white apron with lace on it and held them up. "These are the clothes we wear, and they're called vestments. The black robe is called a cassock, and the white shirt is a surplice. Got it?"

We didn't say anything. "You," he said, pointing at me. "What's your name?"

"Pedro," I answered.

"Pedro, what's this called?" Ricardo said as he lifted the black robe.

"Cassock."

"And this?" He lifted the white shirt.

"Surplice," I said. He nodded.

He handed me the cassock and surplice. "Both of you get dressed. You'll be helping us serve mass."

As we got dressed, Ricardo and José put on their vestments too. Miguel's fit well, but mine were too big. The sleeves of my cassock went a few inches past my hands and the hem dragged on the floor, and the sleeves of my surplice went past my elbows. "You better not step on your cassock," José said, "because if you do, you'll tear it. And if you tear it, you buy it."

Ricardo pointed out Father Bob's side of the closet. "These are Father Bob's vestments. This is the alb, the chasuble, and the stole. Leave them all alone. They're his." He closed the doors.

José opened the refrigerator and pointed to Ziploc bags of crackers. "Those are the host. They're not cookies. Last year we were training two kids to be altar boys, and we caught them eating the host and drinking the wine. We threw them in the canal behind the church. It cost us each a hundred Hail Marys, but they learned their lesson." Miguel and I nodded, fear-struck.

Then they told us that after every mass Father Bob would ask if we wanted popcorn, and that we should always say, "No, thank you, Father Bob."

"But why?" Miguel asked. "He eats popcorn in his house all the time. I've seen him."

"Hey, this is the house of our Lord Jesus Christ, not the house of Father Bob," José said.

"Y también, it makes the church smell like popcorn," Ricardo added. "This is a church, not a movie theater." He went to the front door. "Okay, let's go to the sanctuary and get things ready."

As we entered the sanctuary, we saw Father Bob walking up the center aisle of the church. He was cheerfully humming a tune. I was instantly relieved: Ricardo and José wouldn't dare throw me in the canal while Father Bob was there.

"So glad you two came," the priest said to Miguel and me. "You look like angels in your vestments . . . but Pedro, yours is a little long." He picked and pulled at my cassock. "You can take this home after mass so your mother can raise the hem." He turned to Ricardo and José. "How are they doing so far?" he asked.

Ricardo and Jose nodded, but didn't say anything.

"Well, I guess you boys are doing okay, because you haven't been thrown in the canal yet," Father Bob said with a chuckle. "You'll be fine altar boys. I'll leave you in the good hands of Ricardo and José." Then he walked off, humming again.

Ricardo and José told us not to touch anything on the altar, then walked us around the sanctuary. They said that we'd been to church enough times to know how they did things, and that we should just follow them around during mass and try not to get in their way. "Every time you get into the sanctuary, you must bow or genuflect, understand?" Ricardo said.

We nodded, but Ricardo furrowed his brow and pointed at Miguel. "What does genuflect mean?"

"To kneel?" Miguel said in a guessing tone.

"To kneel," José mimicked. "It means to make the sign of the cross. Let's see you make the sign of the cross."

Miguel tried, but he did it too fast, and according to José, his invisible vertical and horizontal lines weren't straight enough.

"Work on your genuflect," José said.

"And during the part of the mass where we sing," Ricardo said, "if you don't know the words, then keep quiet. I hate it when these stupid people come to church and sing and they don't even know the words." We nodded.

"And during collection, if the rich people who sit up front don't give any money, give them a dirty look and make sure you shake the collection basket in front of their faces. They got money," Ricardo said. We nodded again.

"During the weekday mass, since only the old people come, you two will hold the patens under their chins when they receive the host," José said. "We're sick of seeing their dentures falling out of their mouths."

At six we started mass. We walked slowly behind Ricardo and José from the back of the church to the sanctuary. I gave my cassock a little kick with each step so I wouldn't trip on it. José carried the processional cross, and Ricardo carried the Bible. Father Bob was last; he sang as he walked. When we got to the altar, José stood on one side of the priest and Ricardo on the other. Miguel and I took places next to José and Ricardo. We all bowed and genuflected, then followed the priest around the altar table and stood to his side as he welcomed the people. Then Ricardo and José sat down on the red velvet chairs to the sides of the priest, who sat in the big chair. Miguel and I had to stand the whole hour. We followed Ricardo and José closely, and they didn't say a word.

During the collection part of the mass, Ricardo and José made us carry the baskets. They were attached to long poles, and we passed them back and forth in front of the people in the pews. Ricardo followed me closely, and when this one old man wouldn't give any money, Ricardo frowned at me and nodded, telling me to shake the basket. But I was embarrassed. I pulled back the basket and went on to the next person.

After mass we followed Father Bob to the sacristy and kneeled, and he blessed us, looking proud. He went back out to say good-bye to the thirty or so old men and women who'd attended, and Ricardo and José made us pick up the things we'd used for the mass: the bells, the baskets, a bowl of water, a towel, the processional cross, the patens, and the big Bible. We put everything in the sacristy and took off our vestments and hung them in the closet. Ricardo and José started out the back door, but Ricardo stopped and turned around.

"Hey," he said to me. "Next time I tell you to shake the basket, you better do it. They got money." Then he was gone.

Miguel and I met Father Bob on our way out of the church. "Boys, thank you for serving our Lord Jesus Christ," he said with a smile. "I think you'll be good altar boys."

"Ricardo and José don't seem to like us," I said to him.

"Of course they like you," he answered. "Now, we'll see you on Thursday, and don't be late, because Ricardo and José get mad if people come in late." He walked off, humming a tune as usual.

At home when my mother asked about my first day as an altar boy, I told her I didn't want to be Catholic anymore.

On Thursday Miguel and I got to the church right at five, but again no one was there. We were too scared to go to the sacristy, so we waited until five-thirty, passing the time by studying the stations of the cross. We were talking about how it must have sucked to have to carry a heavy cross and have people throw rocks and spit on you, when Ricardo and José yelled at us. They were standing in their vestments under the big crucifix with their hands on their hips.

"Hey, you're supposed to be getting the church ready!" We jumped in fear.

"Get back here, get dressed, and then get the stuff out," they yelled.

We started walking, but they yelled, "Hurry up!" so we jogged in a panic into the sanctuary.

"Hey," José yelled again. "You don't get in the sanctuary unless you genuflect first. And do it right!"

We genuflected slowly, making sure our lines were straight, and then hustled into the sacristy to get our vestments on. I had forgotten to get mine hemmed, and I stepped on my cassock a couple of times while we put water in the bowl and brought out the bells and the towel. José and Ricardo stayed behind us the whole time, shaking their heads and telling us to hurry.

The priest came in humming. "Ah, boys, it's good to have you back," he said as he shook our hands. "You are in my prayers. Have Ricky and José been helping you?"

We looked over at Ricardo and José, who were standing with their arms crossed. "Yes," we both said quickly.

The mass was better than the last one, because there were fewer people, and when I walked through the church with the collection basket, I didn't have to shake it. Ricardo and José made us carry all the things the priest needed, and I got to ring the bells, with Ricardo cueing me from behind.

Miguel and I didn't mess up at all. After mass Father Bob blessed us, smiled, and patted my shoulder. "Boys, you were great tonight," he said to us, and then he turned to Ricardo and José. "Weren't they?" But they didn't answer. "I think you two are ready to serve at Sunday mass," Father Bob told us before he walked off, humming his tune.

I rode my bike home, excited and nervous about serving on Sunday. I tried to visualize the mass like the sports pros tell you to. I could see myself standing next to the priest, kneeling, and ringing the bells, and I looked good.

I got to the church at nine on Sunday and met Miguel, who was sitting on the bench. We walked right in and genuflected in front of the sanctuary, then entered the sacristy. Ricardo and José weren't there yet, but we knew we had to put our vestments on and get all the stuff out or they'd yell at us. I realized then that I still hadn't had the hem on my cassock raised.

"What do I do?" I asked Miguel, panicked.

"We can put tape on it," he said. "That's what my sister does sometimes." He measured the cassock, held it with his fingers, and put Scotch tape along the bottom. "It looks good," he said.

We finished putting out the things the priest needed right before Ricardo and José came in from the back door. They looked us over and didn't say anything as they put on their vestments.

"You, carry the processional cross," Ricardo said to me. "And you—" He pointed to Miguel. "Carry the Bible. And today *we're* going to hold the patens." With that they stepped back outside and closed the door.

Before mass started we walked out of the church through the back door. Father Bob was there and very cheerful. "Ricardo, José, isn't it a beautiful day, the way the clouds look like feathers in the sky? Angels have wings, you know, and are always watching us." When we walked into the church, there were people everywhere, standing along the back wall and filling every pew.

"It's packed," I whispered to Miguel.

"It's always like this," he said.

"No, it's not."

"Yes, it is, but you and your family always sit up front and you can't tell," Miguel said. "I always sit in the back with my mother, and it's always this full."

The music started and I led the group to the altar with the cross. I could hear some of my friends whispering my name, and I saw my parents on the right side of the church, smiling. My sister covered her giggles as I walked by. When we turned to face the congregation, I spotted all my friends and a couple of my teachers. Mom and Dad looked proud of me, and I wanted to do my best for my family, even though my sister was smirking. The priest welcomed everyone, and they all sat.

Ricardo and José took the chairs, and Miguel and I stood next to them. The mass was going smoothly, and I began to feel the power of being an altar boy. Everyone was watching our every move, and we had a purpose. We had a reason to be there. Without us the mass couldn't go on. We served Father Bob, and we served Jesus Christ our Lord. But while I was feeling all this holy power, I could also feel the hem of my cassock coming undone, and there was nothing I could do except kick it when I walked.

I tried not to look at my friends or family and instead kept my eyes on the clock on the back wall of the church. There were still twenty minutes left in the mass, but we had done everything right so far. When Father Bob had everyone kneel for the Holy Communion, I carried the bowl of water to him so he could wash his hands. Miguel carried the towel, and Ricardo and José kneeled on the carpet, watching our every move.

Father Bob dipped his hands in the water and whispered, "You boys are doing great." He winked at us, and we gave him proud smiles. Then I turned to take the bowl back, and that's when I stepped on my cassock and lost my balance. I could hear people gasp as I began to fall and the bowl slipped from my hands. A slow-motion waterfall took to the air, and the crystal bowl spun rainbows in front of my eyes. I fell to my knees as the bowl broke and the water soaked the carpet.

I could hear some laughing from the church, and I was afraid to look up. Then I felt a shadow beside me, and I turned to see a pair of black cowboy boots. Ricardo put his hand gently on my right shoulder. When at last I lifted my head, I saw my mother and sister, both looking hurt. I could tell they'd trade places with me in a second. But *three* seconds had passed. Ricardo and José stood with their chests out and their hands on their hips. They walked to the edge of the sanctuary and stared down the people. The whole church fell silent, and Father Bob hurriedly walked to me and helped me up.

"Are you okay? Why don't you go to the sacristy? I'll have the other boys finish the mass. Ricardo, take him to the back, please, and José, you take his place."

I followed Ricardo to the back and took off my vestments.

"Now, put the surplice back on and go out there," he said.

"I can't go out in jeans."

"Mira, rule number three: It takes two altar boys to do the mass, and José and me aren't going to do the mass for you guys. Now, get back out there."

We rejoined the mass, and they were at the part where

Father Bob was passing out the Communion. Ricardo walked up to Miguel and took away the paten so he could put it under the chin of a cheerleader.

When mass was over, Father Bob blessed us and told me not to worry about the bowl. "Would you two like some popcorn?" he asked with a smile. Ricky and José scowled at us.

"Oh, no thank you, Father Bob," we said.

Father Bob patted my cheek and walked out to say his good-byes. Ricardo and José followed him, which surprised me. The other two times they had left right after mass. When I got home, my sister told me that Ricardo and José had been out front, threatening the boys who laughed at me when I fell.

"It's a good thing Father Bob was there, or Ricardo and José would have beaten those kids up," she said. And whatever they'd told the kids worked, because the next day at school no one made fun of me.

After a few weeks Miguel and I got the system down pretty well. And Mom hemmed my altar boy clothes to perfection. We still didn't get to sit in the velvet chairs, and at Sunday mass we didn't get to hold the patens, but at least Ricardo and José stopped yelling at us. They'd sit outside and smoke while we prepared the church, and would come in only when it was time for the mass to begin.

"They must trust us," Miguel said with a shrug when I complained.

During Christmastime Santa Theresa was very busy. The big event was our midnight mass, better known as

Misa de Gallo because it didn't end until the rooster crowed. It lasted almost two hours and included a reenactment of the Three Wise Men and Jesus in the manger. I had to be the little drummer boy, and my dad, the chief of police, and the city manager pretended to be the Three Wise Men. I walked down the center of the church dressed in blue and white bedsheets with a pillowcase on my head, gently banging my drum. After the reenactment I sat up in the sanctuary while Ricardo and José served the mass. It was my first time sitting on one of the velvet chairs, and the midnight mass was so long that I eventually fell asleep while everyone else carried on the standing, kneeling, and singing.

In January Father Bob told Ricardo and José that they didn't have to serve anymore, that he was confident Miguel and I could handle things without them, but they said they still wanted to serve the Sunday morning mass. Miguel and I even got keys to the back door of the sacristy, and sometimes we'd come early to throw a football back and forth on the church's lush lawn.

We learned how to serve on all the special holidays: Easter, Good Friday, Ash Wednesday, Palm Sunday, and Mother's Day. And there were weddings, quinceañeras, and baptisms as well. But our favorite was funerals, because we got out of school for them, and afterward Father Bob would buy us hamburgers, french fries, and chocolate shakes.

In May Ricardo and José graduated from high school

and gave up their altar boy duties. After they served their last Sunday mass, Father Bob invited all of us to lunch to celebrate their graduation. Father Bob drove Miguel and me, and Ricardo and José followed in Ricardo's truck. We went to an expensive Mexican restaurant, and Father Bob told us we could order whatever we wanted. I asked if I could have french fries with my enchiladas and Father Bob nodded. Miguel asked if they had ice cream.

"If they have it, you can get it," Father Bob said.

"Can we have beer?" José asked.

Father Bob smiled and ordered Mexican sodas for all of us.

While we all drank our sodas, Father Bob talked about how he wanted the inside of the church painted because the walls looked dingy. "If you boys are willing to paint it, I'd be happy to pay you," he said to Ricardo and José.

"How much?" José asked.

"As much as I'd pay anyone else to do it. You could use the money for college."

Ricardo let out a "Ha!" He looked at José and then back at Father Bob. "We'll think about it," he said.

When the food arrived, Father Bob made us hold hands as he said grace. We got some looks from people, and I wondered whether they felt guilty for not having thanked God for *their* food. I placed my side order of fries in the middle of the table so everyone could have some, and Ricardo and José ended up eating most of them.

"Pedro, how old are you now?" Ricardo asked me, his mouth full of enchilada.

"I'm nine," I answered. "How old are you guys?"

"We're both eighteen—twice your age."

"Isn't that too old to be an altar boy?" Miguel asked.

"Hey," José snapped with a point of his finger, "it's about serving our Lord Jesus Christ. It's not about your age."

"That's true," Father Bob said with a smile. "God doesn't care how old you are as long as you serve the Lord with your heart."

Ricardo and José each took their last few bites of food with quick swallows of soda, and then José looked at his watch. "Bueno, Father Bob," he said. "Gracias por la comida y todo, but we gotta go."

Ricardo nodded. "Sí, Father Bob, the food's good here." He turned to Miguel and me, and said, "You guys are in charge now."

"Hold on a minute," said Father Bob. "I've got something for each of you." He took four small gift-wrapped boxes out of a bag and handed them to us. "Go ahead and open them."

Mine was a silver medallion on a chain. It was about the size of a quarter and was engraved with a picture of Saint Christopher and the words *Protect Us*. Miguel's was the same, but Ricardo's and José's medallions were gold and the size of half-dollar coins.

"I had the bishop bless them, and if you turn them over, you'll see that your names are engraved on them," Father Bob said.

127

"El bishop, eh? Pretty good," Ricardo said. "Real gold?"

Father Bob nodded. "Yes, I melted some of the gold from my teeth." We all laughed politely. Ricardo and José put on the medallions, and Ricardo held his in his fingers for a moment.

"Gracias, Father Bob, por todo," he said. "If it weren't for the church, I don't know where I'd be."

"Sí, Father Bob, thank you for giving us a chance," José said.

Ricardo wiped his nose; his eyes were watering. He gave Father Bob a hug and smiled at me over the priest's shoulder. Then José hugged Father Bob, and he and Ricardo left, waving on their way out the door.

On Tuesday when Miguel and I served, the church walls were bright white. Father Bob said Ricardo and José had painted all night on Sunday and wouldn't let him pay them. He said they'd wanted the money to go toward buying new altar boy vestments.

Miguel and I served hundreds of masses faithfully and even went on trips with Father Bob to the San Juan Shrine to get holy water and sometimes to the bishop's office in Brownsville. We trained other altar boys and even got to play two of the Three Wise Men.

When Miguel turned fourteen, he quit being an altar boy because he'd qualified for a part-time job with the county. It was a state program to give jobs to students from low-income families; they could build their skills by painting curbs, cutting grass, and picking up trash. He still came in occasionally with his mother to clean the church, and for a while he tried to serve on Sunday mornings, but he had to stop completely when he found a second job on the weekends. I became the senior altar boy and had to train all the new recruits and take responsibility for anything they did wrong.

At thirteen, just when I began to understand why it was good to hold the paten under a cheerleader's chin, my father and his friend started a Boy Scout troop. Dad was the assistant Scoutmaster and took me camping along with twenty other Scouts on almost a weekly basis. I began to miss church, but there were other boys to serve, though I had become Father Bob's favorite.

Soon I didn't have any time for serving masses. I camped on the weekends and got involved in school clubs that met weekday afternoons in other towns across the Valley. I also started liking a girl who went to Sacred Heart Catholic Church in Elsa, a town next to Edcouch, and I'd go to her church with her so I didn't have to serve mass at my own. I was fourteen by then, too old to be an altar boy. Miguel had quit serving when he was fourteen, and I wished I could do the same. But I didn't know how to tell Father Bob that I was embarrassed to still be an altar boy.

Then Father Bob was reassigned to a church in a smaller town twenty miles away. Santa Theresa held a fajita cookout on the church grounds as a send-off for Father Bob and a welcoming party for the new priest, Father Salvador. Lots of people who went to Santa Theresa were there to say hello and good-bye. Even Ricardo and José were there, dressed in their usual black T-shirts, jeans, cowboy hats, and cowboy boots. I could see the gold chains around their necks and could make out the medallions through their shirts. They hadn't changed much in five years, and looked just as mean. But Father Bob gave them big hugs, and he beckoned me over to talk to them. We were all there together when Father Salvador came over.

"Father Salvador, I want to introduce you to the best altar boys I have ever known," Father Bob said, patting Ricardo's shoulder. "This is Ricardo, José, and Pedro. These boys have never let the church down." We all shook the new priest's hand.

Father Salvador looked a little confused. "Are you two still altar boys?" he asked Ricardo and José.

"No, sir," Ricardo said. "Pedro is the altar boy now. He won't let you down."

But I did let him down. Father Bob's reassignment was the perfect stopping point for me. I didn't know Father Salvador and didn't feel loyalty toward him. He called the house a couple of times, but I didn't return his phone calls. To play it safe I kept going to Sacred Heart instead of Santa Theresa. Besides, it had prettier girls.

Over the next few years I became even busier with school clubs and camping trips. Church was low on my list of priorities, and since Dad was no longer mayor, he didn't force me to attend. Christmas midnight mass, which our family never missed, was the only mass I'd been to in months.

My seventeenth birthday fell on a Saturday, and Mom told me to go to mass that afternoon to thank God for all he'd done for me. I told her I'd go the next morning instead.

"Good idea," she said. "We go now *and* we go in the morning. Hurry up. Mass starts at four-thirty, and you haven't been to our church since Christmas."

"But, Mom," I said, but buts don't work on my mother.

Only about thirty people were there—all old people, as was typical of the afternoon masses. We sat in our usual spot, way up front, and I waited in the holy silence of the church, listening to the whisper of the ceiling fans and the click of heels against the marble floor. The altar held neither bells nor a bowl of water, and I thought to myself that the new altar boys must be lazy. If Miguel and I hadn't had the church ready thirty minutes before mass, Ricardo and José would have thrown us in the canal.

I began to read the church bulletin and noticed that it now included the names of the altar boys. There were only two boys listed, and I felt sorry for them. No wonder the altar wasn't ready. The last line of the bulletin was the mass intention. It had always been the name of someone I didn't know. But I knew who Ricardo Sangre was.

"Why is this mass dedicated to Ricardo Sangre?" I whispered to my mother.

She leaned toward me and answered, "Because he died a year ago."

"What? Why didn't I hear about it?"

"You were at summer camp," she said. "He was shot."

"How did it—" I tried to ask, but she cut me off.

"Mass is starting," she said, and we stood up.

I could hear the priest begin to make his way to the altar, and I turned to watch. Father Salvador was alone. There were no altar boys to carry the processional cross or the Bible. He stopped and genuflected, then walked behind the altar. With his arms open wide he welcomed us. I turned again to see if there were any altar boys coming, but there was no help for Father Salvador.

Mom elbowed me gently and whispered, "He doesn't have any altar boys."

I didn't say anything and tried not to make eye contact with Father Salvador.

"You should go up there and help him," my mother said.

"Mom, I'm seventeen. I'm not an altar boy anymore."

"Pedro, he needs your help. Go up there," she said in a louder tone.

Father Salvador looked at me, and I turned my eyes down. We sat, and Father Salvador walked to the podium. I lowered my head and kept my eyes to the floor, and then I heard heavy footsteps from the back of the church. Someone was approaching the altar. I turned my head to see a large man in a black long-sleeved shirt and black jeans. He glared at me, and I recognized him through his goatee and moustache: It was José Mata, looking bigger and meaner than ever. He genuflected, then silently walked past Father Salvador and disappeared into the sacristy.

Father Salvador looked out at the few people in the church. "This mass is dedicated to Ricardo Sangre, who served this church with his heart," he said. "May he be in the arms of Christ our Lord."

My mother elbowed me again, but I didn't move. A few minutes later José came back out in altar boy vestments that were too small for him. He was carrying the bowl of water.

My mother leaned toward me again. "Help him. He needs your help. It takes two altar boys to do mass."

José put down the bowl of water and disappeared again. I looked at Father Salvador, who was caught up in his sermon. I stood and approached the altar, genuflected, and walked behind the wall. José was carrying the bells, and he stopped to look at me, but said nothing. He gave me a nod and walked out.

I opened the closet. The cassocks and surplice weren't in order, but I grabbed some and put them on. They fit as though they were mine. I looked in the mirror, genuflected, and stepped out, taking my place in the red chair next to Father Salvador. I could see my mother smiling along with the other old people in the church. A few women were wiping tears off their cheeks.

We served mass quietly, in harmony. During collection I didn't hear José shake his basket, and I didn't have to either. When it was time to take the bowl of water and the towel to the priest, José motioned for me to carry the bowl. I brought it to Father Salvador, and he gave me a pleased smile as he washed his hands. José rang the bells and, like old times, made me hold the paten under the old people's mouths. After mass we kneeled before Father Salvador in the sacristy.

"God bless you, boys," he said to us. "I'll be right back. Let me say good-bye to the people." As he walked off, I remembered the tune Father Bob always used to hum.

José didn't say anything to me. He walked back out to the altar to bring the things in, and I followed. I took the bowl and towel, and he picked up the bell and the Bible. We put everything away, and then José took off his vestments and hung them neatly as I waited.

He turned to me and reached into his shirt pocket, taking out something that stayed hidden in his large hand. He made a fist and put his arm straight out toward me, then gestured for me to hold out my hand. I did so, and he lowered his fist slowly over it. He opened his fist, and I felt something drop onto my palm. My hand automatically closed.

"Look at it," he said in a gruff voice.

I opened my hand and there was a gold Saint Christopher medallion. Engraved on the back was the name Ricardo. José let out a deep breath and nodded, then turned to walk out the back door. I could feel my legs wanting to run after him.

"Wait," I said. He stopped and turned around.

"What?"

"Are you the one who paid for the mass intention?" I asked.

"I didn't pay for it. I made a deal with the priest. I told him I'd paint the church every five years in return for the dedications."

"When are you going to paint it?" I asked him.

"Tonight."

"I want to help."

"It's going to take all night," he said.

"I don't care. I want to paint the church for Ricardo," I insisted.

José nodded. "Okay. We start at six. Don't be late. Ricardo doesn't like waiting." He put out his hand, and we shook on it.